"I believe I have been used unjustly."

There was a moment's delay as he frowned. "What?"

She forged ahead, trying to remember everything she wanted to say. The man moved and put out an arm to her, but she stepped aside smoothly. "I don't know what gave you the impression I was in the market for a husband, but I am not. And you have been lying to me. I won't have it. I won't," she added stubbornly, and paused breathlessly while she tried to finish her thoughts.

"What are you talking about?" Wyatt shook his head, but didn't try to move any closer. "I mean, it's true I went to Mrs. Jessup about her matchmaking abilities, but I hope you'll believe me, my intentions were good. When she suggested I start visiting, I was under the impression you knew about the service. I thought you were happy about seeing me. In truth, I forgot about her matchmaking because I liked you right away."

Annie Boone admits that sweet love stories are a passion. She also enjoys history, so writing about the two together is a perfect match. Adding spiritual elements reminds her of her own faith as she writes. Annie lives in Atlanta, Georgia, with her husband and the two most wonderful cats in the world. She loves to travel, cook for her family and friends, and watch as many sports as possible. Of course, she also loves to read.

The
COLORADO
BACHELOR'S SECRET

ANNIE BOONE

Previously published as *Selina and Wyatt* &
Christina and Mitchell

ISBN-13: 978-1-335-14672-4

The Colorado Bachelor's Secret

Copyright © 2020 by Harlequin Books S.A.

Selina and Wyatt
First published in 2018 by Annie Boone. This edition published in 2020.
Copyright © 2018 by Annie Boone

Christina and Mitchell
First published in 2018 by Annie Boone. This edition published in 2020.
Copyright © 2018 by Annie Boone

This edition published by arrangement with Harlequin Books S.A.

For questions and comments about the quality of this book, please contact us at CustomerService@Harlequin.com.

Harlequin Enterprises ULC
22 Adelaide St. West, 40th Floor
Toronto, Ontario M5H 4E3, Canada
www.Harlequin.com

Printed in U.S.A.

Recycling programs for this product may not exist in your area.

CONTENTS

SELINA AND WYATT

Chapter One

"Remember now, don't be shy about visiting," Susannah called as she waved to the happy couple.

Jeb and Rowena Harbin returned to their cart, and Jeb carefully helped his wife into her seat. It was a lovely sight, the way Jeb's hand lingered on her back to make sure of her safety and comfort before hurrying around to his own seat, picking up the reins and preparing to leave.

They were newlyweds, but already it seemed like they were as close as a couple who'd been together for years. She couldn't resist smiling, watching the younger couple share an intimate glance at one another and then head off home. The sun was setting, and there had been more coyotes running around lately so they needed to be home soon. Fortunately, Jeb was well prepared for just about every situation.

At least, she grinned, she hoped he was. Clasping her hands together, she rested them on her chin and tried to imagine it. The excitement, the joy and thrill of finding out something wonderful was about to happen. That true and abiding love was bringing another soul to the world. That in just a few months, a tiny baby would sleep peacefully in their arms. The Harbin couple was very fortunate.

For over ten years, Susannah Jessup had dreamed of that magical moment. Didn't most girls grow up with dolls? She certainly had rocked them to sleep, taught them to walk, and fed them carefully at supper time. How many times had her own mother instructed her to put the doll away at the table?

Only a few short years ago she came to the realization there would be no swelling of her belly, no moment of wonder when she found out there was a child forming within her. No babe would be born into their family who would look like her and her husband. That dream of hers would never become a reality.

The door creaked open, the only sign she received that he was near. Lucas walked so quietly, he could often surprise her with his touch before Susannah even knew he was nearby. While her senses were good for living so far from town, Lucas Jessup had spent years as a Texas Ranger perfecting the art of silent movement. He enjoyed testing his abilities.

A small sigh escaped her lips, and she leaned back once she felt his presence was near enough to her. He caught her easily, moving forward and slipping his arms around her where their hands rested on her flat stomach. Her throat constricted as the Harbin couple, soon to be a family of three, disappeared around the curve of the hill.

Lucas rested his chin on the top of her head. "Are you mad at them?"

Her smile faded, and she knew it was a fair question. They'd gone through so much, and this didn't make things easier. But how could she be upset at the young couple? After everything Rowena had gone through? Slowly, she shook her head and tried to imagine such a thing. "Of course not. They deserve to be happy and I truly am thrilled for them."

With his chest against her back, she felt him breathing against her, deep breaths out in the fresh air. It was another minute before Lucas spoke again. "Does it make you sad?"

Her breath caught when she thought of her answer. The simple response would have been a lie, and she couldn't lie to him. He'd know the truth, anyway. Thoughtfully she closed her eyes and tried to gather the strength to tell him, but the words were difficult to pull out.

"I'm happy for them," she managed finally, trying to avoid the question. "They deserve happiness, Lucas."

Stepping back, he tugged on her arm and tried to wrap her in a proper hug, but Susannah deftly side-stepped with a shake of her head. Biting her lip, she dropped her gaze and turned towards the house. Though he was reaching out to her, she couldn't welcome his embrace, not like this. The pain in her heart was heavy enough that being near him would only make it worse.

This deep sadness didn't creep in often. She was happy. She loved her husband, and he loved her. They'd both made peace with their childlessness. They filled the void with people in need and each other.

"We're happy." Lucas followed her into the house. "At least, I hope you are." The last part was meant to be a joke, and she could hear it in his voice even as it fell flat between them.

A bitter smile came to her face as she headed towards the kitchen. "I know, Lucas. I know."

Though she was hoping he would catch the message she was trying to send his way, the hint she was finished talking to him, Lucas didn't get it. That, or he understood and simply didn't accept it. "It's what you wanted," he insisted. "You wanted to play matchmaker so they could be married and have families. You wanted this to happen."

"I know."

"And you let old sadness surface when they're doing just as you wished," Lucas continued. "You can't do this every time one of them gets married and starts their family. It goes against all the reasons you wanted to do this. You can't just—"

Trying to ignore him, she picked up a pan hoping to return to cleaning up the kitchen from their supper, but Lucas wasn't the sort of man who could be ignored. A sudden burst of frustration hit her, but she couldn't listen any longer.

"I know!" She slammed a spoon so hard against the table it clattered out of her hand and skittered to the floor. The loud bang after her yell silenced them both immediately. Lucas jerked back, a hand instinctively dropping to where he usually kept his guns, and Susannah stared at the spoon on the floor.

Her hands were hanging loosely at her side, but suddenly she realized they were shaking. Whether it was anger, anguish, or something else, Susannah wasn't certain. All she knew was Lucas was only speaking the truth even if the truth was made of pain.

Most of the time, she was satisfied with the direction life had taken her. It had required time and much prayer to get here, and sometimes she just wanted to forget the truth. Apparently, this was one of those times.

Cautiously she glanced up at Lucas, uncertain of what to expect from him. It had taken him a while to come to terms with their childless existence, too. It had been a hard time for them both before they had accepted all of it. Yet somehow, she knew, her barren life was something she couldn't get over completely.

As much as she reminded herself she truly was blessed and fulfilled as a wife, she couldn't stop the envy that crept into her heart. Whenever they visited Eleanor and Matthew with their two girls, and all their friends who already had children or were preparing for them like Jeb and Rowena were, she felt empty. Yes, Susannah wanted them to be as happy as possible, for she truly believed each one of them deserved it.

She took great joy that her emptiness had brought them together. For if she had children, she wouldn't be a matchmaker. She wouldn't have time to help lonely hearts find each other.

She was beyond blessed herself to have Lucas as her husband. He'd stayed by her side after learning she'd never bear his child, something not every man would have done. She was thankful for him every single day.

Lucas's gaze was not of anger, as she had feared, but rather of melancholy. It was the feeling trapped within her ribs, and just looking at him reminded Susannah he still struggled with it, too. It reminded her she wasn't alone. And that had to be enough. Gathering her breath, Susannah inhaled deeply and composed herself.

He reached her side, carefully taking one hand and

then the other in his larger ones. Though she wanted him to wrap his arms around her, Lucas waited as she swallowed the lump in her throat.

"I'm fine," she mumbled finally, sniffling. "Oh, dear, I'm sorry, Lucas. I don't know what came over me. I didn't mean to yell at you." Gritting her teeth, Susannah glanced down at her hands held firmly in his. "Really need to focus on the better things—the perfect things in our life. There are so many good things. It's hard to do otherwise. Rowena is going to be a wonderful mother. And Jeb, he's already so good with children. They're always running to him after church, you know. He races them and lets them win. Who knows? Perhaps she'll have several more after, like the Mendels. They have twelve children now, isn't that right?"

Lucas's hand brushed against her shoulder lightly. "You're rambling."

"I know." She gave him a tight smile. "I'm trying to focus on the blessings, Lucas, on what we have. Not what we don't and will never have. You'd think after all this time I'd handle it better all the time—not just some of the time. I'm sorry."

She had hardly finished the second apology as he wrapped her up in his arms. For a moment she resisted since he hadn't done it right away. And part of her didn't want to be comforted since it wasn't a fix to the problem.

But his warmth melted everything else away, and Susannah could feel the love emanating from her husband. Soon her own arms wound around him, and he didn't pull away until she was smiling lightly. "Thank you."

He kissed her forehead. "That's what I'm here for." Lucas winked at her and helped her clean up the kitchen.

The tightness in her chest slowly faded away as they both knew it would. Her breath came easier, and after some of her husband's playful singing, Susannah could smile again. The man was a good singer, and he knew music always brightened her mood.

Perhaps it was best, she decided, the last two girls had been here only two months before marrying men in Colorado Springs. Hillary and Brooke were lovely girls, ready to be married. Now Olivia was nearly due with her first child, and Rowena was expecting one as well. It might be good for her now to have some time to herself, time to focus on her home and on her husband.

Chapter Two

Wyatt, 1873

"**I** can do it!" He stamped his foot, only realizing too late he sounded like he was six years old, not sixteen. But in a world like this, he could already be considered a man—just as he should be. Balling up his fists, he glared at the man squinting at him from his high horse.

Clearing his throat, the young boy set his shoulders back and gathered his pride. "I can do it," he stated more calmly. The other man had hardly twitched during their conversation, and Wyatt Thomas wondered how a man could act so calm and collected. Even after what he had seen the man do, Luis the Sixer hardly looked phased. And that's what Wyatt wanted. "Whatever you need me to do, I know I can do it. I know how to shoot, how to throw a punch. I can even do the laundry and cook," he added, a hint of desperation in his voice now. "I need to get out of here, and I can learn to do what you do."

Luis the Sixer stared at him coldly for a good minute. His handlebar mustache never budged though he could hear the man's nose whistling as he breathed. A hand on his pommel, the other was hidden beneath his jacket. A knee jerk reaction, surely, since Wyatt had stepped out from behind the barn and caught him off guard.

His was an old jacket, too, one made of animal hide. He didn't know what sort of animal, but clearly a dead one. There were two bullet holes on the left shoulder, but Luis didn't act like it had happened recently. Luis hid his face beneath a wide brimmed hat, but that part was ridiculous since it didn't really matter who saw him. He was a bounty hunter. He went after the hunted. He was a strong man who could beat a man unconscious and shoot another at the same time if necessary. This was evident to the two men tied to Luis the Sixer's packhorse.

"What's your name, boy?"

Swallowing with a gulp, Wyatt tried to stop his hands from shaking. He wasn't afraid, he just hated not being in control. "Wyatt Thomas. And I'm not a just a boy anymore." He just prayed he could calm down and control his uneasiness before the anger took over.

"It's a hard life, Thomas. Some nights you won't sleep, and most nights you won't even have a proper bed. It's a beautiful life of seeing the different towns and land, but it's hard and it's long and far from cozy. You think you have what it takes, boy?"

"I do." He held his head high. "I have it."

The hand came out from beneath his jacket holding nothing and he stroked the big black mustache. "Can you shoot?"

"Real well."

"Oh yeah?" He felt the hardness of the gaze and Wyatt hesitated.

"Well, some. I hit my target as long as they stand still."

The man snorted. "That won't be your targets." The hope that had been building within his chest faded, and Luis's horse stamped his feet as though they were ready to be on their way. Without him. Gritting his teeth, he stared at the ground angrily, wishing the man would just decide already. It was humiliating.

"Fine." The bounty hunter had to say it again for Wyatt to understand. "Fine. Get your stuff. You got a horse?"

Grinning, Wyatt nodded and jabbed his thumb behind him. "I do. That one." It had been his father's horse from ten years ago. A beautiful creature, even in his older age. While he most likely wouldn't last more than the next few years, Wyatt had still treated him well enough to keep going and stay strong. A big black horse, nearly twenty hands high, and so persnickety that no one else could ride him.

Luis whistled. "All righty then, boy. Let's get going." Wyatt knew the man was watching him as he grabbed his pack and strapped the horse up, ready to go. In his haste, he had to redo the straps twice on his stirrups before finally getting everything as tight as it needed to be. He was red in the face, scowling by the time he climbed on to the horse.

And they started off on their journey.

That evening, they rode for several miles before settling down in their own campsite on the edge of West Virginia. Luis got the men off his packhorse and tied the animal to a tree as Wyatt tried to get the fire going.

He had done it before, and he knew how to do it. But the sticks he rubbed together weren't doing what he wanted. If anything, they only splintered. Sweat dripped down his forehead and Wyatt scowled at the setup before him, angrily trying to make the flames come to life. "Come on," he muttered. "Spark!" Giving up, he flung the branches out in front of him.

Only for Luis to appear from the shadows and catch the one pointed at his chest. Wyatt leaped back, having thought he was still alone. "Watch it." The older man glared at him. "You're not the only quiet footer here. Don't ever think you're alone, kid. And don't think we're about to eat this raw." In his other hand he held a bird he had caught, the neck already wrung. "Try it until you get it."

"It's not working." Wyatt glowered. "It won't work. I can't get it to spark."

Luis scoffed, eyeing him. "It ain't wet so nothing's wrong with the stick." He took a seat on the rock after flinging the stick at Wyatt. He had caught without even glancing at it, glaring still at the man before him. It was more arrogant than impressive. He talked with such ease, mocking the younger man. Mocking him for his efforts? Wyatt was trying to help, and this was the thanks he got?

"What do you mean by that?" He gritted his teeth and stood. "Huh? You think I'm good for nothin'?"

But the man hardly looked his way, tending to the feathers on the bird. He plucked them lazily, one by one as he bit down on his pipe. "I didn't say that, boy. Why? Do you think you're good for nothin'?"

"Why you lousy—" His hands clenched. Wyatt went in for a punch, the adrenaline pushing him hard and the anger steaming from every pore in his body. After all, it was the better move to be the one to throw the first punch. It had been effective in most of his fights. A few times he'd even knocked the other man unconscious within the first few jabs.

But Luis raised a hand and deflected it as though

the young man were only a fly. Unfazed, he pulled out another feather as Wyatt nearly fell forward, catching himself just in time before trying to throw a second punch, this time with his left.

With a sigh, Luis stood and grabbed Wyatt's left wrist, twisting it away in one motion that immediately caused a burning sensation along the muscles from his fingers to his shoulder. Wyatt cried out, falling to his knees helplessly. "You ain't getting nowhere with an attitude like that, boy." Luis gritted his teeth, using a tone that instantly quieted the young man. "Especially out here with me. Men who talk like that are likely to disappear, you get what I'm sayin'?"

Wyatt looked at him with contempt but kept his tongue.

"Now you're going to get up, pick up those sticks, and try again. I don't care how long it takes you, but you'll get that fire going so we can eat. Thomas, you're not to say another word this evening or even look my way if you expect some of this supper. Then you'll go to your bedroll and wait for tomorrow. If you want to make it to tomorrow, you need to rethink your strategy. Nod if you understand me."

Locking his jaw, Wyatt angrily tested moving his arm, only for more pain to shoot up through his shoulder. He couldn't escape this hold no matter how he tried and grudgingly knew there was only one way out. For a minute he glared down at his other hand, still in a fist, unable to accept how helpless he was in such a sparse amount of time. Red-faced and panting, he finally nodded since he didn't have another choice.

"Good." Luis pushed him away. Wyatt fell on his other arm, getting that whole side of him filthy in the dirt. Stumbling up, he tried to clean up and turned to Luis while thinking up every mean thing he could think but remembered what he'd agreed to do. He hesitated.

He couldn't beat the man, he knew this was true. Swallowing, he went back to his spot to obey and tried to consider his options. But he wasn't a liar, Wyatt told himself, and shouldn't start now. It was one of the longest evenings of his life, trying to get the first fire going. But eventually the kindling caught. So he had something to eat and he went to bed.

During the night, he had the same dream all over again. A memory that had turned into a nightmare, the dream that sent the rage coursing through his body and constantly woke him. Ten years ago, his parents had gone into the bank and six men followed them in. The six men were the only ones to come out, running off with everyone's money. And their lives.

It hadn't helped that Wyatt had to go live with his brother on the outskirts of Philadelphia. Luis was easier to handle than what was left of his family had been, and that was one of the reasons he'd just left them for good.

But Wyatt was right, and he could do it. He learned to skin the animals and light the fire in record time. Luis made sure he could take a punch and give a better one back. He taught him how to fire on a moving target. While his father's horse only lasted another year after riding all over the countryside, Wyatt Thomas worked hard to bring justice to the world and became a bounty hunter. The anger had built inside him for years and was finally used for good.

Chapter Three

Selina, 1883

The shout made her jump. "Stop looking at yourself and get back to work!" Glancing behind her, she found Aunt Mary glaring from the back porch. Mary was a short woman, frumpy with too much hair piled on top her head. Flour covered her skirt and apron as she cooked. And as usual, she was in a huffy mood. "You heard me! Stop wasting your time! Don't let the laundry get ruined." Then she disappeared through the door.

Sighing, Selina wished it were the other way around. Glancing at her wet raw hands, she wondered if they could possibly be any redder. Most likely not. Pursing her lips, she curled them into balls and hoped they would heal faster than they did last week.

She gave her reflection in the river one more look before grabbing the basket of laundry. It wasn't that she was looking at herself, but rather looking for a glimpse of her mother. Having lost her nearly fifteen years ago, Selina Carlson knew the memories of her parents were dim but she hoped that by squinting at every corner of her own reflection, she might be able to see either of her parents. Just to remember them better. It was her grandmother who'd said she was the spitting image of her mother, with her father's eyes. But the woman had told her little else.

This wasn't a good idea, she knew, to dwell on dreams and one what couldn't be. The last eight years with her aunt and uncle had taught her it was a cruel world.

Her arms ached as she carried the wet laundry back up the hill to the house, wondering once again why the path wasn't good and flat. She certainly walked it enough, bringing the water buckets for the house every day and for the laundry and the cooking and the cleaning. It required several trips and it never grew easier.

"Don't hang it so crookedly! If you do it that poorly again, I'll make you start all over!"

The threat was a good one, and Selina had suffered those consequences before. Several times, if she remembered correctly. She no longer winced at the shouting but frowned at the job she was doing hanging the clothes on the wire. What was she talking about? After years of practice, she knew to hang the wet laundry as straight as she could.

Just for good measure, she took the last three shirts she'd hung down, and rehung them. They were exactly the same as before, but doing the work over didn't garner a shout from the kitchen window. Selina shrugged it off and focused on completing her task. Picking up the pile of damp hand towels, she put them on her shoulder so she wouldn't need to keep bending over, and carefully picked out the clothespins from her apron pocket.

She'd only hung one up when a tingling sensation ran up her spine. Something felt wrong.

Biting her lip, Selina glanced about, wondering if someone was looking her way. But she couldn't see anyone and unnerved as she felt, she turned back and hung up another towel before looking around again. The nagging sensation of being watched continued to bother her, making her hair stand up on end. She was looking around once more when someone finally spoke.

"Your blouse is wet."

Jumping, she stifled a scream by clasping both hands over her mouth. There, just beyond the oak tree, was her uncle James Robinson. He was a tall man, one who had once been very strong but now spent more time eating and the softness showed. Hunched with dark brooding eyes, he looked worn down like the devil was on his back. Her heart hammered as he came over, eyeing her.

"Excuse me? I'm sorry, I didn't hear you," she murmured, dropping her gaze from his uncomfortable stare. He did that often these days—the staring and watching. She should have known it was him. Since their foster son, Ben, had left to work on the railways four years ago, things had been different. Without Ben around, the shouting had grown into a daily event, and tension filled the house from dawn to dusk.

He gestured towards her chest. "You're wet. The towels." Stepping closer to her, he was still staring at her. Wondering what intrigued him so much, she glanced at her blouse and saw he was right. The damp hand towels had made a damp spot on her clothes. The blouse stuck to her skin now, showing more of her curvature than any decent woman would have ever intended. Instantly she turned bright red and grabbed the towels, holding them in front of herself.

"Ah," she stammered finally. "I should go change and then I'll finish the chore."

But he grabbed her arm before she could leave. "No, that's all right. It's a warm day. The sun will dry it."

She nodded obediently, knowing it was better to obey without question than talk back to them now. Selina waited, expecting him to leave. It was only after she turned and stared at his arm on her that her uncle finally pulled away. James stepped back a step and leaned against the tree.

Taking a shaky breath, she realized he wasn't about to leave. He was settling in. Self-conscious she glanced at her top again, wondering if he truly intended to… but what was she to do? For several heart beats she just stood there, dreading the moment she got back to work.

"Selina! Get in here! I need an extra hand. Leave the laundry for now!"

Aunt Mary didn't need to ask her twice. The hand towels went back into the basket, and Selina wrapped her arms around herself as she ran into the house. Uncle James was left behind, standing there in the shade. The stove was a two-woman job, and the laundry was finished once Selina's shirt was dry.

The looks didn't stop, but Selina tried to be more careful about her clothes. While most of her things were old and too small, she did what she could to be quieter and smaller, hiding from James's leering. She thought she was being careful until one day, nearly a month later.

Most days she started her mornings off carrying four buckets of water from the river to the house. When she returned with the first two, she found James and Mary arguing heatedly in the kitchen about running to the store for more flour. She claimed they had enough, but he was telling her it had ruined in the night. Selina thought nothing of it until she brought the next two buckets in and found Mary going out through the front door.

"I'm off to the mercantile. James is getting ready to leave as well. Get the bread started with what flour we have left and make sure you clean up your mess. I want the floor nice and tidy when I return." There was no chance for Selina to say anything as she watched the woman head down the road.

She wasn't often left alone since Mary preferred to stay home. Besides, she told herself, there was no reason to worry since James would be heading off to work as well, in the factory. Stepping inside, she set the buckets down on the table and went to put one in the sink just as she heard footsteps coming up behind her.

He was right there as she turned, startled at the sound of creaking floorboards. James stepped up close, close enough that their hips touched even though she leaned back against the sink. Her breath caught as she met his gaze with her wide eyes, trying not to shake. Disgusted and petrified, Selina tried to think. Gripping the counter with all her strength, she found darkness in his gaze, a hunger that sent pure unadulterated fear through every nerve in her body.

"Finally. Took us long enough to be alone," he scowled, and grabbed her around her waist.

"Wait, no," she gasped, clumsily trying to pull free. The looks had been enough though she could have endured that. She'd ignored his gawking for years. But he was touching her, and the unfamiliar and greedy grips made her shudder as she tried to push him away. "Please, don't!" Her breath strained as she felt his mouth on her bare neck and tried to squirm free.

She yelped as he bit her ear. "Don't think you haven't wanted this," he huffed, shoving her hands away. His breath was hot against her as he found her lips, pushing himself against her. Writhing, Selina frantically looked for any weak points before finally getting a hand in his face, and she kneed him in the gut.

The man grunted, and she cried out as his teeth ripped her lip. As he clutched himself, it left her just enough space to step to the side and run. Touching her lip, she saw the blood come away on her fingertips and glanced back. To her horror, James was leaning against the door, staggering after her. Selina turned back only to run into the laundry line.

Crying out, she found the blanket fall over her, trapping her. Gasping for breath, she stumbled and tried to escape the folds. "Please oh please oh please," she cried out, finally free but already she heard his heavy breathing much nearer now. She turned towards the river, hoping to dash across it, only to have her hair yanked and Selina fell backwards.

James clumsily grabbed at her throat, his dirty nails scratching her as she kicked him hard on the shin. But he was a big man and hardly winced, barely phased. "Shut your trap," he ordered her. "I don't have much time." But it only made her move more quickly, shaking as she fumbled to free his grip on her braid.

That's when he released her neck and walloped her hard in the stomach. It was like a boulder hitting her, and all the breath left her body. Selina doubled over in pain, clutching herself as she tried to fill her lungs once again. Before she could do so, he grabbed her wrist and twisted it. Forced to stand, she gasped and found his fist headed for her face. She ducked, but she wasn't fast enough and he hit her on the shoulder.

With her uninjured arm, she tried to do the same and punch him in return, but Selina knew she was weak and James sidestepped her easily, shoving her away. She nearly toppled over, but managed to stay upright. Still wheezing, but she didn't see his kick soon enough and fell to the ground.

"Just because you're pretty doesn't mean you can do whatever you want," James grumbled and kicked her.

Selina cried out, her eyes watering. "Please! Please stop! Stop it, please." She put up her hands in defense as he crouched over her. For a moment she clung to the hope that he'd help her up or at least walk away, but he only slapped her face. The man crouched and his knee dug into her hip. Her leg went numb and she couldn't break free. He continued to beat her, even after she fell unconscious.

Chapter Four

"We need this, we need that. More sugar, more flour." Mary mocked her husband's grumbles on her way home, scowling at the items in her arms. It had been a ridiculous request, she decided, having her leave the house so early that morning for items they didn't even need yet. The man knew little about keeping house, and less about the kitchen.

It was a good home, at least, she tried to remind herself. And she had a warm bed and a roof over her head. That wasn't something she'd had all her life, and it was a decent street to live on as well. A few homes even sat near the river. It would be a good home if her husband would ever finish painting it. Mary glared at the door, half brown bare wood and half white.

But the last time she had told him he needed to finish his work, he had smacked her hard with her own big serving spoon. It made her hand smart at the thought of it and she shifted her hold on the bags. "Dirty man," she scowled beneath her breath. "I don't care if he brings home the money, he could still be neater about his work."

Huffing, she made her way inside and set the shopping on the kitchen table. Mary stopped there, glancing around and wondered why it was so quiet. Suspiciously looking around her, she looked for the bread the girl was supposed to have made by now, and found nothing. She sniffed the air and only smelled an empty house. "Can't even follow the most basic orders. I knew I should haven't left that lazy child behind."

Without the bread, it would ruin their evening meal and it would set all their chores behind schedule. Now there wouldn't be enough time to make the butter, and they still had to preserve the fruit before it was too ripe—and there was already a chance it was too late. Mary reminded herself for at least the tenth time she'd never take in another niece or nephew again.

Even the laundry was still out, she could see it out the window. The bedding swayed in the breeze, tugging this way and that. Mary went to the sink with pursed lips, already planning a good scolding for Selina.

Leaning forward to get a better look, she realized there was a bare spot between a skirt and a pair of trousers. Something was missing. Most likely a piece of clothing that would now need to be rewashed. She gritted her teeth at the thought of double work.

Selina wouldn't sleep that night, not if she had something to say about it. She would wash up and make the bread no matter how long it took.

"Where is she, anyway? Well, at least she brought the water in." She muttered lowly, glancing down at the wet droplets. But on the rim of the sink, what she thought was water, came away sticky. To her utter confusion, Mary realized it was blood. For a minute she stared.

"James?" she called out uncertainly hoping he would answer and explain.

But he should be off to work. Even she had heard the factory bells peal out the start of the shift. These outskirts of town, most of the folks worked in one of the three factories and they didn't allow for slackers. He had to be at work, or he wouldn't have a job.

Selina wasn't here, either, at least not as far as she could tell. "Selina? Girl?" She waited, glancing around. As she stepped back, Mary looked around for more blood, finding only a small dab of a blood fingerprint against the door jamb leading down the hall to the back door.

Following it, she found the door hung halfway open. She pursed her lips. James must have left it ajar since he had a way of slamming the doors so hard they popped back open. "I must talk to him tonight. Though we have already discussed this several times already." Shaking her head, she frowned at her silly fleeting idea that fussing at him again would fix the problem.

Mary had only taken two steps outside by the time she found more blood, this time wiped on a hand towel. "What on Earth!" She looked around frantically at what could have possibly happened while she was away. The wind moved the laundry line, and on the other side she saw something out of place and hurried over.

Selina laid there in a collapsed heap, still and silent. At one angle, she looked as though she were sleeping. That was until Mary grew closer. She was covered in scratches from her ankles all the way up to her face, and blood was on her face. Mary's hand flew to her mouth in horror, her stomach churning.

At first, she wondered how this could have happened,

but as she fell on her knees beside the girl, Mary realized there were handprint bruises forming on young Selina's neck. How often had she hidden her own bruises? It hit her like a pile of bricks—or more like a well-placed punch from James. She knew exactly what must have happened. Faint, Mary touched her niece, trying to see if she was still breathing.

Her face twitched, the face that had always been so pretty with a sloping nose and hazel eyes. The girl looked like her mother, who had been the looker of the two sisters. Mary sighed in relief, realizing she was alive. But only just.

"What have I done?" She realized only then how bad everything was, and hurriedly tried to raise the girl's head, rolling the towel and placing it beneath her head. "Hush, hush, child, hush." Tears spilled down her face as Mary scrambled up, and she ran off to find the doctor.

James had a temper, something she had always known, and feared. But it was just the way of life, she thought, since she knew their parents had some issues in the past when she was a child herself. People got angry and did things, but they didn't always mean to do them. Did they? Mary shook her head, clasping her hands together.

She sent a neighbor for the doctor while she waited with her niece. When he arrived, he saw Selina and shook his head. "How did this happen, Mary?"

"I'm not really sure, Dr. Koop. I found her this way. Someone must have tried to break in."

He looked at her with a raised eyebrow. "You sure?"

Mary's eyes filled with tears and she shrugged. She couldn't tell the truth and risk making James angry.

"Well, let's get her over to the office. She needs more attention than I can give her from here."

They took her to his office with the help of her neighbor and his cart. Dr. Koop and his nurse closed the door behind them leaving Mary alone in the small, plain waiting room. Pacing, she tried to stop her shaking hands and think things through.

How did I let my anger and frustration control me? Why did I stop paying attention to what was going on? I should have done more for Selina. She's my niece, and I had an obligation to my sister. Selina didn't deserve this.

Mary's sister, Selina's mother, had found a man who hadn't hit her. She was a soft girl, much like their mother who had managed to outlive her husband for several years. Until she had come to Mary and James, Selina had never been treated so cruelly, Mary was certain. Yet she had never said a thing. She'd allowed James to hurt the girl and never once tried to stop it. She wanted to scream at her own weakness.

"She doesn't deserve this," she told herself tearfully, and then angrily wiped the tears away. Showing tears was a terrible failing after all. Nobody liked it when she cried. Mary had never been pretty, and her skills had eventually landed her a husband. So she tried to make herself neat and tidy and did the best she could to make James happy.

She couldn't let this go on any longer. Licking her chapped lips, Mary turned to the newspaper on the nearby table and tried to distract herself. She hoped some idle reading would help her sort everything out.

As Mary browsed the adverts, she found the solution. It jumped out from the page and she couldn't ignore it.

In Rocky Ridge, Colorado, there was a boarding house just for women. The people there assisted women who wanted to find husbands. This seemed to be a better strategy with a matchmaker involved rather than hoping it worked out with a stranger. The advert promised cheap board, the ability to learn, and a safe home.

A safe home.

That was it. Mary jumped up and clutching the newspaper, she ran back to her empty house. Breathlessly, the woman grabbed what she could find and went to her wardrobe where she found the small bit of savings she'd been hiding from James over the last couple of years.

Please let this be enough. She counted it several times as her heart pounded in her chest. Hurriedly she scooped the coins back up into the coin purse and bolted out the door.

"A ticket to Colorado, please," she told the train master at the train station. "To Rocky Ridge, that is."

The man hardly looked at her. "Closest stop is Colorado Springs. Next one leaves tomorrow."

She nodded, glancing around anxiously. She hoped Selina would be well enough to travel by tomorrow. "All right. One ticket, please."

Chapter Five

Her whole body ached. From head to toe. Selina wanted to submerge herself in the darkness again, but something tugged at her memory. Her Uncle James's face flew into her mind.

Leaping forward with a gasp, she opened her eyes wide and searched around her looking for him. Someone grabbed her arm, and she cried out in pain, trying to push them off as she squinted in the bright light. He was still there, Selina thought desperately, and tried to fight him.

"Calm yourself!" An unfamiliar voice proclaimed in her ear, and she froze in surprise. Shaking, Selina felt her strength fade as she collapsed backwards. It was a cot, not the yard. Blinking hard, she swallowed hard and looked around her.

The light was so bright. Too bright. Only then did she realize they were talking to her. She raised a hand to rub her eyes, but they stopped her gently. "Miss Carlson, please. You're safe, you're all right. And don't touch your face, you don't want to hurt yourself."

The more they talked, the more she could see the two figures hovering over her. There was a man and a woman. The man was young, sallow, and had the bushiest eyebrows she had ever seen. In contrast, the woman was older, heavyset, and wore her thin faded red hair tied back. It was difficult, Selina decided, trying to discern what they were thinking.

"How do you feel?" The woman patted her hand kindly with an almost indulgent smile. "You've been sleeping for nearly a full day now, Miss Carlson."

She winced at the touch and carefully lifted her hand to find it wrapped in a bandage so firmly she didn't even know what the injury looked like. But Selina could tell it was bad. Then the memories started coming back to her. Uncle James had grabbed her wrist and twisted it. Shivering, Selina fell back. Now she recalled how James had touched her, had hit her, had hurt her.

She was safe now, right? She glanced around the room. "Where am I? Who brought me here?"

The woman glanced at the man and nodded approvingly. "I told you she looked like a sensible girl. Let's get her some water, shall we? I'm sure she's parched." Giving the man a pointed look, she gestured to the table nearby.

He huffed something about being the real doctor but obeyed, stepping away and filling up a cup of water. Trying to be patient, Selina watched the strangers and waited anxiously for answers. But the water came first, and she suddenly realized how thirsty she was.

They waited until after she drank all the water and then the woman spoke. "My name is Ellie Monson, and that's my nephew, Dr. Reid Hathaway. Isn't he charming? He's doing a very good job here, and he has an excellent practice set up. You've been here since yesterday morning."

Selina closed her eyes slowly and breathed in deeply.

"You're injured. Your aunt didn't say how it happened, but it was quite a terrible accident." Ellie paused to pat her arm carefully.

Selina reached up to touch her lip. It felt odd and it hurt.

"I wouldn't do that if I were you, dear. You've got so many bruises and that's a nasty cut on your lip. If you're not careful, it'll split again and I wouldn't want stitches there." Ellie reached out and gently eased Selina's hand away from her face.

"Perhaps you should rest." Dr. Hathaway glanced at his aunt, waiting for her approval.

The woman shrugged. "Let's get her something to eat, shall we? She must be starving. Can't you see how thin she is? Bring it over. No, we'll do the cabbage later. Just the soup, dear. Thank you. Miss, let's get this in your belly, shall we? Reid, help her sit up."

Selina sat up and cautiously accepted a few mouthfuls as she looked around the room one more time. It was only then she noticed there was a small table beside her bed and just below it, a familiar bag. She squinted her eyes to get a better look and sure enough, it was an old bag kept in the back of her closet. Not since she had used it to bring her belongings with her from her grandmother's had she seen it.

"What is my bag doing here?" She swallowed hard. "I don't remember bringing it here. I didn't have it before."

Chuckling, Ellie shook her head. "Of course not. No, dear, your aunt brought it. She said you would want your things with you. Would you like to see them? Perhaps it shall bring you some comfort, I think."

But the doctor tutted. "Now, now. This is too much excitement, Aunt. She should get some rest. She has enough injuries to keep her in bed for a month, and I don't want to risk us ruining the healing process."

Ellie just waved him off. "It will help her sleep. Here you are, dear."

A peek in the bag proved she was correct. Her belongings were inside it. Everything she owned.

But why? Are they throwing me out? This is the only shelter I have. No matter how horrible it is, I have no other place to go.

Then she noticed the envelope folded inside. She pulled it out and opened it up with shaking hands.

Dear Selina,
Your mother wanted better for you than I have given you. I have been wrong to treat you so poorly. And it has been even worse to allow my husband's molestation. This is the last thing I can do for you, to protect you. When he comes home, he will wonder where you are, but I will deal with that as best I can. I don't want him to hurt you again. I'm sorry I was not strong enough to do this until now.

There's a boarding house in Rocky Ridge, Colorado, that takes in women. You will be safe there, far away from here. You'll find a few coins at the bottom of your bag. It's all I could manage and I wish it could be more. Go to the boarding

*house and ask for Mrs. Jessup. And forgive me
if you can.*

*Yours,
Aunt Mary*

After reading it three times, Selina was still uncertain. A train ticket sat in her lap and she picked it up. The destination was Colorado Springs. And it was leaving today. Today.

Inhaling sharply, she jerked her head painfully about, looking for a window. They said she had been sleeping here for almost a full day. She could hardly believe a day had gone by since she'd been bringing in the buckets of water and working on laundry.

"What time is it?" She demanded. "I have to go."

"Go?" Ellie blustered. "It doesn't matter what time it is. You can't possibly think of such a thing, dear, not in your state. Why, you're injured. For all we know, moving too much could hurt you even more."

But Aunt Mary's words made sense and Selina grew antsy. Grabbing at her bag, she pulled out a scarf. "Please, I have to, I must go." It was her only chance to escape this place. She had to get away from him.

"Now listen here," Ellie started sternly.

"No!" Selina cried out with a vehemence that surprised them all. "I can't stay! This wasn't an accident, you must understand. I can't be here where he can find me. He might kill me."

For several minutes they tried to assure her of her safety. But as exhausted as Selina was, she knew her aunt was right and she had to go. They weren't happy for her to leave but the doctor and nurse finally conceded.

"This is how we're going to do it," Dr. Hathaway decided. "Aunt, you'll drive her to the station. I have Mother's old cloak, and it has a hood she can use." He turned to Selina and stared for a minute. "I'll find you a bonnet, as well. In the meantime, my aunt can make sure your bandages are fresh and you must eat the soup for strength. Understood?"

The women nodded. While Selina focused on getting the soup down, Ellie explained how she should care for her injuries. Eventually Dr. Hathaway returned, providing her the extra clothes and a small bag for the herbs and medicine. He helped them to the carriage, and they started the drive to the station.

She had been awake for hardly four hours before Selina stepped onto the westbound train. Clutching the ticket, Selina used the last of her strength to find her seat. She nodded to Ellie who waved farewell.

Leaning against the window, she took a deep breath and stared at the ticket stub in her hands. Everything had happened in such a flurry, and her head was spinning. Closing her eyes, Selina prayed that whatever came next would hurt a little less.

Chapter Six

The house had many windows, a wide porch and sat on a huge plot of land. All the pathways leading from the house were clear and outlined with rocks all the way to the barn, the road, and the pasture. With the river and barn just before the mountain, only the northeast entrances would allow guests. Lucas had made sure no one could come upon his ranch without his knowledge.

Wyatt Thomas believed in being prepared for everything even if it had been a few years since he'd left the business. Luis the Sixer had died a gruesome death soon after they'd gone their own ways, and that's not how Wyatt wanted to go. Besides, over the last few years, his anger had faded and the pent-up energy had found enough justice and vengeance to last him a lifetime.

Now, he just wanted the life his parents had started. Wyatt wanted a home, his own land to work on, and a family. The last idea struck his mind again as he helped a tall, round-bellied young woman down the steps.

She had soft red hair and beamed at him as they reached her wagon. "That's the one," she said breathlessly. "Thank you, I appreciate it. I shouldn't be out and about being so close to the baby's arrival, but Simon keeps forgetting things. So I had to make sure we bought flour this time. Would you mind checking on him? My husband, he's just inside."

Shifting, Wyatt couldn't help but glance at the large belly again. Clearly, she was with child, but few were out and about in town so near their delivery time, or at least he'd never seen a woman walking around who was about to bear a child. Returning his gaze to the woman, he nodded and returned inside, immediately finding the only man who was alone.

Simon noticed him before he arrived and tipped his hat. Wyatt nodded in return. "Your wife is outside," he stuck his thumb towards the door. "I was on my way in and she headed to your wagon."

"What?" Simon's eyes widened in concern. "Where is she? What happened?"

Wyatt shrugged. "She was fine. Wanted me to remind you about the flour."

"The flour?" The man looked at him in confusion before it dawned on him. "Oh, flour. Yes. Why, I haven't even looked for that yet." He found it just at the end of their aisle. Wyatt watched as the young man picked out a large sack and hefted it over his shoulder. "Thank you, um, I didn't get your name."

Wyatt fiddled with his hat. "Wyatt Thomas. I'm pretty new to these hereabouts."

Nodding, Simon appraised him. "Right. Not completely new though. I've seen you around the church, haven't I?" He grabbed seeds and walked to the register. For some reason, Wyatt followed him, glad to have a conversation with a man and not his cows.

"Right," Wyatt informed him. "I've been here nearly a year, but I don't get out much, I'm afraid."

Simon gestured with his elbow towards a bag of sugar. "Do you mind?" Wyatt shrugged and picked it up as they walked. "Thanks, Thomas. Well, Rocky Ridge is a good place to settle, that's for sure. I have everything I need right there." He looked at his wife and turned back with the biggest, foolish grin Wyatt had ever seen. "Have you got yourself a wife?"

He shrugged, glancing around the store. "No, not at this point."

"You should try it sometime," Simon offered. "It changes everything, more than I expected. Have you met any of the girls around town?"

The former bounty hunter eyed the other man carefully. "You're trying to play matchmaker?"

Simon laughed. "Maybe. After things went so well with Susannah and the boarding house, it's hard not to want such good things for everyone. Loads of folks here know about it. Haven't you met the Jessups?"

Lucas Jessup, the sheriff. That wasn't something he would forget. Every bounty hunter had a complicated relationship with the law. The first thing he'd done when he arrived in Rocky Ridge was to study the sheriff to figure out if they would have any trouble. But the man was said to be honest and respectful, a former Ranger who could do what he needed in times of trouble.

He shrugged. "Not really."

"The wife, Mrs. Jessup, she's a matchmaker and boards young ladies while helping them find a husband. The Jessups are a great couple. You should talk to them sometime, see if they have a lady for you."

It was as if he was saying Wyatt could shop for his

own wife, and he chuckled at the absurdity. Shaking his head, he picked up the sugar again for Simon and carried it out to the cart. They found Mrs. James there, petting the horse and she beamed more at the flour's arrival than her husband's.

"You're such a gentleman," she assured Wyatt. "Thank you for all your help. I'd make you supper this very minute, but I'm of little use in the kitchen lately. After the child comes, you must come visit us."

He tipped his hat as Simon helped his wife onto the cart. "Anything you like, ma'am. That's very kind of you. Take care." He gave a short wave as they parted ways, for he had work to get back to.

Simon's words struck him. The idea of using a matchmaker to find a wife was odd, but it sure would increase his odds of finding someone. But then the worry of having a wife and a family would come back all over again. What about his past? How much could he let go of? He wanted to be free of the bad memories and hard life.

By the time Sunday arrived, Wyatt had decided to give Mrs. Jessup a chance. He needed the good to outweigh the bad in his life, and he couldn't do it alone. He told himself this over and over during the sermon, eyeing the sheriff and his wife. Perhaps no one would be a suitable match, but it couldn't hurt to try. He hung back in the shade as he watched the blonde woman greet everyone after the sermon. Mostly, her husband stayed mostly quiet by her side.

Until he came for Wyatt. The bounty hunter sensed him once he was close and turned as Lucas Jessup silently stepped out from around the corner. He had moved his sheriff's badge to the folds of his vest so it wouldn't glint in the sun. Though he'd attended church with everyone else, the sheriff still held two guns around his waist. He had even removed the clasps, Wyatt noted.

"Good afternoon." Sheriff Jessup nodded cautiously.

Fighting the urge to reach for his own gun, the younger man nodded curtly. "Afternoon, sir."

The man went straight to the point. "Any reason you've been watching my wife since church started?"

Wyatt liked the approach because it saved wasting everyone's time. "I have watched her, indeed." He knew he shouldn't lie. The sheriff would see right through it and he wanted to make a decent impression. It wasn't in his best interest to dodge the obvious. "And you, too." Lucas's shoulder twitched at the revelation and Wyatt fought back a grin. "I've been thinking about settling down, and your wife's services have been mentioned."

The tension eased immediately. While Lucas remained restrained, he locked his guns back into place. "Ah. Well, that's all right as long as you're looking for a wife. You can't have mine," he added with a smirk. "But I'm sure she'll be of help. Would you like to speak with her?"

"If it's all right by you," Wyatt stated politely.

Lucas put out a hand. "Of course. I'm Lucas Jessup, by the way."

"Wyatt Thomas." He accepted the sheriff's hand and the two men shook.

But Lucas didn't let go. "Wyatt Thomas? The bounty hunter?"

He hesitated and nodded. It was a life he owned up to. One that had been as good as it had been bad, but it was mostly rough and unkind memories. He wouldn't complain since this was the path he'd chosen. "For-mer," he added. "I'd like to be done with that life, if you don't mind."

The man gave him a long measuring look before stepping away. "I know what you mean. Come along. I'm sure Susannah will be more than happy to talk with you. And you didn't have supper plans, did you?"

Wyatt raised his eyebrow as they walked out of the shadows together. "No, I hadn't thought that far yet."

"Then let's go on and plan for you to come out to our place. Susannah will likely not have it any other way." Lucas nodded and then headed towards the pretty blonde who would possibly help change Wyatt's life.

Chapter Seven

Humming, Susannah Jessup bounded around the kitchen trying to clean up her mess. "At least Lucas won't be home for a few hours," she murmured, glancing at the large bowl of berries. "And at least the pie is good."

She glanced at the plate on the windowsill. The sugar on top sparkled in the sunlight and her stomach grumbled. Frowning, she turned back to her utensils and put everything in the sink. Once the kitchen was tidier, the lack of clutter allowed her mind to focus and she turned to the pork roast. Supper was her priority.

She was stoking the fire in the stove when she heard something in the yard. A cart? Susannah frowned, unable to recall if Lucas had taken the wagon into town. Curious, she peered towards the window but saw nothing.

"He'll come in eventually," Susannah decided, and focused on the task at hand. It would take hours to cook the roast at a low heat and could be easily ruined if she wasn't careful. Once the meat was in, she went to the sink to wash her hands.

She looked out the window and saw Lucas on his way to the house. But he was moving slowly and had his arms wrapped around someone. Frowning, she squinted and tried to see who was with him.

When they got closer, she realized it was a young woman, struggling to walk on her own. Immediately Susannah jumped into action. Dropping everything, she hurried to them. "Lucas? What's happening? Is she all right?"

For a moment she had wondered if it was an older woman. But the bonnet hid a face years younger than her own. The girl was injured and clearly in pain. Sucking in a breath, Susannah shook her head and went to the girl's other side. "Let me help," she said urgently, and her husband stepped back to open the door for them.

"Thank you," the woman murmured.

Susannah considered settling her at the table since it was so close. Except it was a mess, and far from comfortable.

"Lucas, take her up to the room next to ours. Just pick her up. That'll be easier and faster."

He nodded and picked the girl up and took the stairs two at a time.

Susannah's mind buzzed with so many questions. She knew she'd get the answers she wanted soon, but now it was time to take care of the girl.

Lucas placed her gingerly on top of the bed. Susannah pulled her boots, cloak, and bonnet off as the girl collapsed beneath the blankets. Her eyes closed even before Susannah tucked the blanket around her.

"Oh, thank you so much." The girl sighed. "I've brought the money to pay you for my room. It's in… Um, it's in my bag."

Lucas stepped forward. "Her bag's still in the wagon. I'll get it." He left hastily.

Licking her lips, Susannah glanced back to where her husband had disappeared, and then to the girl. She was pretty, even beneath the deep scratches and her cut lip. It looked puffy, just like her black eye.

"What shall we call you?" She gave her a tentative smile, wondering if she'd give her real name. Not that Susannah would know the difference, but she was obviously running from someone. Leaning forward, she unpinned the girl's dark hair and ran her fingers through it lightly.

"I'm sorry, I haven't even introduced myself. Forgive my poor manners, please. My name is Selina. Selina Carlson."

Offering the girl a smile, Susannah nodded. "It's a pleasure to meet you, Selina. Don't worry about a thing. Just rest for a while, and I'll bring you some porridge, shall I?"

She wanted to say more, but the girl was already fading. Only by letting her know she was safe would Miss Carlson rest easy.

Susannah watched Selina fall asleep. For a minute she stood there, hands uncurling the young lady's hair, wondering anxiously what had happened. She had seen the broken way the girl walked, and the bandage on her wrist. The girl wore a blouse with a high neck and Susannah worried about other unseen injuries.

Tomorrow, she told herself, she'd see to the young girl. Susannah turned and found her husband standing there with an old carpet bag. For a moment she considered rummaging through it, but finally set it by the bed untouched before closing the door.

"Where did she come from?" she whispered, wrapping her arms around her middle. "Whatever happened to her? How did you come to find her?"

Lucas said nothing as he wrapped his own arm around her on their way back to the kitchen. "I was at the train station. You know how I like to watch people come and go. She was the last one off the train, wearing her bonnet and cloak as if it were winter." He shook his head and tightened his grip. "She didn't say much when I asked if I could help her. She just said she needed to find the Jessups. So, I borrowed a wagon so she could lie down and thought it best to come straight home."

"It was best." Susannah nodded her agreement with his choice. "You did the right thing. But the poor girl. Do you think someone hurt her or was she in an accident of some sort?"

His chin rested on her head. He waited a minute to respond. "Definitely appears to be scratches from someone's fingernails. Her lip was probably split when someone hit her." She shuddered, and he tightened his grip on her. It was a horrible idea. "But she's safe now," Lucas reminded her and leaned around to kiss her cheek. "We won't let anything terrible happen again."

Swallowing, Susannah nodded. "Do you think someone's after her? What if they come looking for her?"

"Could be, but there's no way to know until they show up. I can handle anyone who needs to beat up a woman, though."

Susannah took in a deep breath. "I know. And I always feel so protected with you. I'm grateful for such comfort, Mr. Jessup. Oh, I mean Sheriff."

Together, they stood together in a warm embrace for several minutes until they finally returned to their duties. Susannah began to clean up the kitchen, and Lucas needed to return the wagon to Dr. Fitzgerald. When he came home for the evening, they ate the pork roast but were so distracted it was difficult to enjoy.

Perhaps it was a good thing, Susannah decided, she never slept much. She couldn't imagine resting while this girl was suffering. Twice during the night, she stepped out of her room and went to the young woman. On one trip, she took the uneaten bowl of porridge and brought more water. The second time she placed a cool cloth on her forehead.

The next morning, Lucas headed to town, and she was preparing oatmeal to take to Miss Carlson. As she was serving it up in the bowl, she turned to see her limping into the kitchen. Selina looked exhausted as she leaned against the table and tried to smile. Susannah hurried to her and held out a hand to steady her.

"Oh gracious. I didn't hear you come down the stairs. Sit, sit, please." She pulled out a chair. "There you are. Now what are you doing out of bed?"

"It's already morning." Selina hesitated as she looked around the room taking everything in. "I'm sorry to be a bother. I didn't know where to go. I mean just now after I woke up. Coming here to your boarding house was my plan all along. You are Mrs. Jessup, aren't you?"

Sighing, Susannah sat beside her. "Yes. And you slept fairly well in a boarding house bed last night. You can stay here as long as necessary. But dear, I really don't think you should be out of bed yet."

The girl shook her head. "No, that's all right. I feel much better, truly." She tried to smile, but the cut on her lip started to tear.

Pulling out a handkerchief, Susannah sighed and

dabbed at the blood. "Careful, dear. Are you hungry?" But the girl said nothing, only offering a helpless shrug. Susannah brought the oatmeal and placed it in front of Selina. "Here you are. Eat it all if you can. You need to regain your strength."

Obediently the girl picked up her spoon, but glanced at her damaged hand and frowned. Susannah watched as Selina gingerly put the spoon in the other hand and awkwardly tried to scoop the food into her mouth. "Oh, this tastes like manna from Heaven."

"Good, good. Now, Miss Carlson, let's get things sorted out, shall we? We'll talk expenses later and I can give you a tour when you feel up to it. Here at my boarding house, we all work together. I'm only assuming you don't intend to go back to where you came from, so I'll teach you the skills you'll need to keep a home. Where are you from? Well, that is, if you're ready to tell me."

"Boston, ma'am."

Selina didn't volunteer any more information about her home, so Susannah decided to leave it there and learn more later. She nodded and hoped she was being supportive enough to help her talk. "What did you do with your time in Boston?"

The girl talked slowly. It sounded as if she did very little cooking, but could do nearly everything else fairly well. As Selina talked, Susannah noticed she avoided mentioning family or her life. One look at the black eye made her decide not to pry. The girl had been through an ordeal, there was no doubt about that. She would focus on healing and teaching her skills. Talk of marriage could wait until later.

Chapter Eight

At first glance, Susannah Jessup seemed like a confident woman who was kind and caring. When her hair was down, she looked like a princess and when she ran around in the garden, she looked like a mother hen. Selina marveled at the woman who had left that morning to take care of her business in town and then came home to a burned pie and smoke-filled kitchen. She rushed around to clear up the mess.

"She did it! It happened!" She opened the door as she balanced a bulky box of potatoes. The plan was to get them to sprout and plant those in their garden. Selina stared at the unstable box, willing it to steady in Susannah's grasp. She did wonder what the loud enthusiasm was about and wasn't sure why Susannah didn't notice the smoke hanging above their heads.

"Who did what?" Selina was curious and couldn't contain her question.

Susannah put the box down and twirled over, clasping her hands together. "Olivia! She's had a baby girl, can you believe it? Oh, I hope the dear child has Simon's eyes. I wonder if she has dimples. The midwife just came into town since Olivia is doing well. She had the babe late on Sunday last. I knew it was just about time when they didn't make it to church. I'm so thrilled."

Her enthusiasm was irresistible, and they forgot the burnt pie for several minutes. Susannah hummed and bobbed her head until Lucas arrived with another box he immediately put on the floor. He chuckled at the sight and shook his head. Though she'd been with them for a week, it was the first time Selina saw Lucas smile spontaneously. His eyes never left his lovely bride.

Then he went to her and held out his hand. She took it with a giggle and he twirled her around the room. They made up their own song as Susannah continued to hum. Lucas was a little stiff but Susannah's fluid movements made it hardly noticeable. Selina's heart pattered, and she smiled. It hurt her lip, but she could see clearly now and she clapped along to their tune. After two turns around the large kitchen table, Susannah twirled one final time before dipping into a curtsey, and Lucas returned it with a bow.

Sighing joyfully, Susannah took a deep breath and glanced back at Selina, smiling because of her enthusiasm. "Well, next Sunday we're hosting a supper for them—Olivia, Simon, and the baby of course. I stopped to talk to her before coming home, and she said she's sure she'll be fine to come for supper. There'll be a few more friends, and it's going to be lovely." Susannah Jessup was in such a good mood she didn't even care the pie was ruined.

It had been a happy moment, and eventually they got back to their duties. Life went on, and Selina took things slowly. The Jessups were nice even though she ignored the probing questions. It was hard to explain her past, Selina decided, and thought it best to put it all behind her and focus on the possibilities ahead of her.

Already Lucas had promised to teach her how to ride a horse and how to milk a cow. She worked well enough with the laundry and cleaning, but had little experience with animals and cooking.

Mrs. Jessup insisted Selina prepare the rabbit stew for the supper party. Her hands shook as she butchered the rabbit and put the pieces in the pot.

"Just be slow and steady with your cuts. No need to be in a rush." Susannah's voice was calm and trusting, yet Selina wasn't sure why.

"You know I haven't ever cooked anything successfully. I did mention that, didn't I?"

"Yes, a time or two at least."

"So, why do I need to do this? And for so many people. Can't we start this part later? I have no doubt it will be a disaster." Selina continued to cut the rabbit into pieces as she tried to convince her teacher to take over.

"You're doing wonderfully. I couldn't do it better, so there's no need for you to stop. You do want to be able to cook for your family one day, yes?" Susannah tilted her head and raised an eyebrow waiting on the answer even though it was obvious.

"Of course. You're right. I have to learn sometime."

"Indeed. Might as well start now. So now chop the vegetables and put them in with the rabbit. After that, we'll be ready to put it in the oven."

At last it was Sunday, and Selina was enjoying the festive mood in spite of her recent flight from a family who didn't care about her. Everyone was happy and smiling, enjoying the company of friends. She looked around curiously, trying to imagine being part of a close group. Sitting by the window, her gaze drifted away towards the setting sun.

"Miss Carlson, isn't it?"

Glancing up, Selina found Olivia standing there, free once again of the baby. It looked like Eleanor had the child now if she remembered the names correctly. Hesitantly Selina nodded and watched as the woman joined her on the soft seat. Sharing a long sigh of relief, Mrs. James closed her eyes as Selina watched curiously.

"You have the best seat in the house. Truly. I don't want to ever get up from here." Olivia's eyes glazed over as she looked out at the soothing view.

She sighed again and Selina turned her gaze away, embarrassed. Usually she'd been twisting her hands by now, but she'd needed to stop the nervous habit with her still injured wrist. Healing was taking longer than she'd expected and she was growing tired of being sore and physically impaired.

Today they'd been so busy preparing for the party she hadn't taken a nap. This change in routine since she'd been attacked had made her ill and exhausted. And the more tired she grew, the more the pain made its emphasis on her body. She glanced at her wrapped up wrist and wondered yet again when it would heal.

"You came from Boston, didn't you?" Selina watched Olivia uncertainly while her eyes were still closed. Was she imagining things? But then she opened her eyes and repeated the question, and Selina took a deep breath.

"Yes," she whispered, watching Jeb and Lucas laugh at something. It must have been something to do with their jobs because both Susannah and Rowena frowned and the men hastily changed the subject. "Boston. The outskirts, really."

Olivia James shifted her pillow carefully. "I'm from Vermont. Simon is from around Boston as well. He doesn't dwell on it much these days, but I often wonder if he ever misses it. Do you?"

"No," Selina shook her head. "Not at all." Swallowing and trying to breathe evenly, she blinked and recovered. "That is, not really. But I haven't been gone too long."

The baby woke up and started to fuss. Eleanor tried bouncing her gently, but Olivia was ready for her. Her exhaustion left behind, the new mother stood up but paused, glancing at Selina. "I didn't know what to expect when I came here, either. But I promise, it only gets better from here. You couldn't be any safer or better prepared for a new life than here with the Jessups." She winked and went to check on her fussy, groggy baby. Her husband got there at about the same time she did and hovered over them protectively.

Her husband had a gentle touch, Selina noticed. It was one of the most touching moments she had seen in her life. A lump formed in her throat and she wrapped her arms around herself, watching the new little family as they strolled away to have a moment of privacy. It was touching to see such love between them for their child, and it took all her strength not to burst into tears.

Their little family was so different from what she had known. She hardly remembered her parents, and her grandmother had been good to her but quiet and distant. With her aunt and uncle, it had gotten so much worse. Her bandages and pains were part of her old life and she wanted nothing more than to forget about those days.

Who was she to be surrounded by good and happy people? Selina wanted happiness and comfort, but she'd never had it. Because of her inexperience and awe at these precious moments, this made her wonder if she was pretending to be part of them when she never could be. This should be an opportunity to start over, but how was Selina to change if her past still held her in its jaws?

"Are you all right?" Eleanor paused. "Dear, your lip is bleeding. Here, let me help." She felt around inside her pockets before pulling out a handkerchief. It was soft white and trimmed with lace. "What happened?"

It was a long story, and a shameful one at that. "Thank you," Selina murmured, and shook her head. "I don't know what happened. But I'm fine. I'm all right."

Eleanor looked confused then she nodded. Suddenly Selina was thankful for people who didn't pry too far into her business. She didn't need a busybody reminding her constantly of her sordid past. She was ready to move on and she hoped she could get help from these people.

Chapter Nine

Selina, 1879

It was the middle of harvest season, and she felt desperate for a delicious apple pie. She was young and bold, not afraid to ask for what she wanted. She'd risen early and dressed at sunrise. Once she had braided her hair, she decided she had waited long enough.

Skipping out of her tiny room, Selina hurried to the kitchen and cooked breakfast. The food grew cold before her grandmother staggered out into the hall, leaning on her cane. "You were up early. I could hear you."

The girl blushed. "Sorry for waking you, Grandmother. I couldn't sleep. The early morning is the best time of the day, isn't it? That's what you always say."

"Selina." The elderly woman sighed and brushed her long hair back. "There's a point where it's too early. There is still much for you to learn, my girl."

Nodding furiously, the girl glanced at her plate, and then at her grandmother's food. "Yes, of course. Did my mother get up early when she was my age?"

But the woman didn't answer. She focused on cutting her egg, a task made difficult with her aged and shaking hands. There was little she could do these days and usually spent the afternoons in bed. She used to do needlework for the town, Leesburg, just outside Philadelphia.

Selina had come to her as an orphan when she was five years old. Her parents died in an accident, innocent bystanders turned victims in a shootout. She remembered very little of the time and Grandmother wasn't talkative enough to share the details.

"She was smart, wasn't she?" Selina was hesitant to ask too many questions, but today she was bolder than usual.

"She was a good child." Her grandmother picked at her food. "Did you wake early because of your dreams?"

The girl flushed and glanced away, wishing she hadn't mentioned the dreams. Children in town would make fun of her if they knew she was afraid of the dark and the sounds that always came with it. More than once in the last month she'd woken from her night horrors screaming, and it was the only time Grandmother showed she cared.

Tall and prone to jumping at sounds herself, she was there the moment the little girl cried. She would wrap another blanket around Selina and croon a lullaby. She whispered calming stories in her ear, and Grandmother would assure her she was not alone and that she was safe.

Selina sniffed. "No, Grandmother. I slept well last night. And you know, I was thinking. Since tomorrow is my birthday, maybe you could tell me more about my mother. And we could make an apple pie," she added hopefully. "I could pick the apples in the orchard."

Her grandmother was excruciatingly silent and took two more slow bites. Selina fidgeted, unable to sit still. She shoved breakfast into her mouth, wondering if Grandmother needed the question again. "Will you let me go?"

Grandmother sighed, a heavy one that made Selina close her mouth immediately. She might have been quiet and frail but there was no fighting her if she had her mind made up. "You may pick the apples. We should use them all before they go bad, anyway."

Selina nodded hurriedly and cleaned up before grabbing up her bonnet and the basket. "Of course! You're completely right, Grandmother. Why, we could even make two pies, don't you think? I'll be back as soon as I can!"

It wasn't quite an orchard since most of the trees were dead and Grandmother only owned five on the corner outside their house. But when she called the five trees an orchard, it felt as though things were better than they were. Selina clung to the hope that something good would happen soon.

Late afternoon arrived before she knew it, carrying every good apple in her basket and one in her pocket. There had been two others, but Selina had eaten them. They weren't the best ones, so it wouldn't matter if they weren't in the lot for later. Humming, she hurried back to the house.

"Grandmother, I got all the apples from your orchard!" She hurried into the small cottage anxious to show her grandmother something that would make her happy. Swinging the basket, two of the ripe apples tumbled out and scattered across the floorboards. Hastily little Selina set the basket on the table and ran around on her hands and knees to find the lost treasures.

They were both bright red and hardly bruised upon her inspection. She was satisfied and after giving them a good rub, she set them back in the basket. "Grandmother?" she called out in the silence, looking about.

When she didn't see her grandmother in the room, she

glanced back to the sun to find it was definitely later than she'd realized. She was likely in trouble for being away so long. There were crocheting needles and yarn on the bench by the window, but her grandmother wasn't there.

"I suppose she's napping. It's that time of day." Selina bit her bottom lip and looked around again. "I guess I could cut up the apples. That might make her happy."

She prepared the apples and decided to continue. After a few years, she knew the apple pie recipe by heart and soon had the pie resting in the window to cool down. She stood looking at her work and wondered about her Grandmother again. She went to her room and knocked on the door. It wasn't closed, so she peeked her head in, finding her Grandmother lying still on the bed.

In that moment, somehow, Selina knew that her grandmother was gone. Swallowing, the little girl tip-toed across the room and touched her grandmother's hand. It was cold.

Selina felt a lump in her throat. Her breathing was suddenly too loud, and she bit her lip. Had she cried when her parents died? She wished she could remember. Though she couldn't quite recall what they looked like, sometimes she remembered the way they smelled or the love in their hugs.

Grandmother had never hugged her, at least not that Selina remembered. She'd been standoffish and quiet. Selina had learned to speak and walk carefully though sometimes she forgot as she had earlier in her excitement about the apples.

Standing quietly looking at her grandmother, she didn't know what to do about the loss she suddenly felt. She'd dealt with loss before, but it felt different now.

Tears trickled down her face as Selina carefully rose and put her cloak on. She tied her bonnet and fixed her shoes, then stepped out the door. Keeping her head down, she crossed town and asked for directions until she arrived at the physician's office. It took the rest of the morning, but she finally made it.

"I think my grandmother's dead. I found her sleeping and she won't wake up." Selina looked at him steadily then wiped her drippy nose on her sleeve.

"Are you sure? I imagine she was overly tired. Go home and give her more time to rest. She'll be fine then." The doctor looked down at her with kindness, but he seemed certain she didn't know what she was talking about.

"No, you need to come. She needs you."

"Well, then. Let me get my bag." He nodded and went to the other room. Soon he was back with a bag. "Let's go and check on your grandmother."

They went out the back way to his cart. He helped her up and got in beside her and slapped the reins to get his horse to move.

"My house is out by the dry creek." Selina felt nervous and hoped she'd done the right thing by leaving her grandmother alone while she came for help. "I hope you're right and she's awake now."

"We'll soon see, child."

They soon arrived and Dr. Collins jumped out of the cart and rushed in. Selina followed close and then watched as he touched her grandmother's neck and then her wrist. It didn't take long and soon he shook his head.

"I'm sorry. Your name is Selina, right?"

She nodded. "I was right?"

"Yes, I'm afraid so. Get what you need and you'll stay with my family tonight. I'll sort out the details with the sheriff."

Selina felt lost and alone, but she was thankful for

his kindness. Mrs. Collins planned a small funeral and Selina said goodbye to the only family she had left.

"Are you Selina?"

She was keeping the doctor's children happy with their marbles in the front yard and hadn't even noticed anyone near enough to speak to them. A young man stood just inside the gate with his hat in his hand. He had floppy brown hair and a smile that made his eyes crinkle. She nodded hesitantly, and he put out a hand.

"I'm your cousin, Ben."

"Cousin?" She stood with a frown. "I didn't think I had one."

He shrugged. "Well, Mary and James aren't my real parents, but they took me in when I was younger. They call me their son once in a while so I think that's close enough. James sent me to take you home. We should be going."

Mrs. Collins came out and confirmed she was expected to go live with her aunt and uncle. She was bewildered and forlorn at how her life had changed again so fast.

"My grandmother never mentioned any other family. I'm not going with a stranger."

"I guess we should have prepared you for this, Selina." Mrs. Collins watched the man named Ben for a moment and sighed. "Mary is your mother's sister. I don't know why no one told you about the rest of your family, but you do have blood kin."

Selina stuck her chin out and thought for a moment. She looked up at Ben and then away again.

"You belong with family, Selina. I'm here to make sure you get there safely." Ben stepped to her and held out a hand.

Deciding she had no other option, she stood up and took his hand.

Mrs. Collins helped her get her things into her bag and packed them a basket of food for the road. Soon she was headed to Boston with Ben. He'd borrowed a second horse, and the two of them made good time.

She asked as many questions as she could think of on the journey. Ben was patient and kind, answering every question she threw at him. Selina wondered what her aunt and uncle were like. All the answers in the world couldn't take the place of seeing for herself and she was anxious to get there.

Would they be cold, like her Grandmother? Or perhaps cheerful like her cousin was?

Finally they arrived at the place she would soon call home. Ben held his hand out for her and she took it as they went through the door. "I'm back! Selina's here!"

"About time." The tone was disgruntled and rude. Selina jumped when a cranky looking woman met them in the kitchen. "Get us some fresh water, will you?"

Selina glanced at Ben who shrugged. He was a happy fellow, so different from this woman who must be her Aunt Mary. Her heart sunk.

For the first week she asked questions about her family, but they had no interest in the past or helping her understand more. Selina's curiosity slowly died. The hope in her heart dimmed. The only reason she didn't lose her optimism completely was because of the small Bible Ben handed over one night.

"You asked me what makes me happy. It's this book. Everything you need to know is inside."

"I can't read." She looked down and pushed the book away.

Ben sat down beside her. "Then I'll teach you."

Chapter Ten

Susannah, 1883

She shook her head at the young woman, trying not to be exasperated. Once again she was left wondering what it was with Selina why she was so stubborn and quiet. Susannah wished again she knew Selina's story. It would help to know where she was really from, why she clearly never slept well, and what had happened to her. Knowing the details of the beating might make it easier to help her.

"I don't care what you want," she repeated. "You're going to town with me to see the doctor. You've been limping since you arrived and I want to make sure nothing serious is causing it. Besides, I'm sure he would like to look at your wrist. I know there's something wrong with it since you keep favoring it. I see more than you think I do."

As she talked, Susannah bustled about the room. Since they were heading into town for the day, a last minute plan, the women would need to take care of the chores before they left. Tending to the animals, the garden, and getting supper started had to be finished before they could go.

Though she appeared to be unafraid of hard work, Selina had stopped at Susannah's mention of visiting the doctor. What could have happened that she was so self-conscious of her injuries? Selina worked hard on all the chores she was responsible for, and Susannah wondered if the work on top of the injuries was making her worse. At this point, the young woman might need to be resting between every chore—or not doing any chores at all.

"Oh, that's not necessary." Selina hesitated and waved the idea off with her good hand.

"Oh yes, it certainly is." Susannah opened the curtains and gave the girl a firm look. "I will have Lucas carry you to the cart if we must. But I don't allow problems to go unattended for too long. In fact, I should have taken you to Dr. Fitzgerald's the first day you arrived. Here we are." She pulled out a dress from the girl's wardrobe. "We have a busy day ahead, so let's get started."

Humming, she moved about the house in her usual orderly fashion. They had yesterday's bread with some fresh butter and jam for breakfast. After tidying up the kitchen, Susannah joined Lucas with the barnyard animals. By the time they finished, they found Selina watering the last of the garden.

Soon they were on their way into town. Selina was quiet, and Susannah wasn't surprised as she'd expected her to be annoyed, or at least worried. Lucas helped them out of the cart when they arrived at Timothy Fitzgerald's office, and Susannah led the younger girl inside.

"Well, if it isn't our very own Susannah Jessup. What can I do for you today, ma'am?" Timothy wouldn't be Timothy without his loud drawl and bowler hat. He tipped it towards the two women as he wrapped up a conversation with his wife, Alice, who was dropping off a basket.

"Good morning," the woman said softly and left them to their task.

Susannah put a hand on Selina's shoulder and looked at the doctor. "I have a dear friend with me and she's had some trouble. I'd like to make sure Miss Carlson here is doing all right."

He nodded, waving his fingers at them. "Of course, of course! Come, step right into my office. This way, ladies." The short man led the way down the hall.

Dr. Fitzgerald was a friendly man who had been raised on the road by his parents who had been doctors as well. His sister worked as the midwife for the area, a good team of two cheerful and rather loud folks. They were very likable, and Selina would soon see there was nothing to fear.

"Miss Carlson, where do you hail from?" he asked as he opened a room for them. There was a cot and three chairs. Susannah glanced in and then stepped aside for Selina who entered and took a chair. Susannah followed, and the doctor took the last seat.

It didn't take long at all. While Selina refused to explain anything, the tension was ignored by both Timothy and Susannah by their positive approach to get the truth. Susannah sighed at the difficulty, but they were eventually able to sort through the majority of Selina's injuries with Timothy's attentiveness.

"You've survived quite the bashing," he told her.

"But you're healing well, I can see. Your eye will be right as rain soon enough, and I don't think your face will scar. It'll just take a little time. Your ribs will heal a little slower, but your breathing should be fine soon enough. Your hip is our only real concern. Did a horse fall on you?"

Susannah glanced quickly over at Selina who offered a tight smile at the joke. "No, fortunately." Her tone was hushed and uncooperative.

Timothy didn't mind and shrugged. "Well, it's all right. Time should help it. Get some rest and you'll be back to normal before you know it. Let's re-wrap your wrist before you go. Other than that, we'll be done here."

Selina was quiet as Susannah finished her conversation with Dr. Fitzgerald and then they stepped back out into the sunlight. Clasping the younger girl's hand in hers, they started down the street for the mercantile.

"I know you didn't care for the visit with the doctor, but I feel much better knowing with a surety everything is well. I don't want anything ill to happen to you, and you've been quite tired since you arrived. But Dr. Fitzgerald is right, dear, you clearly need more rest. We'll end our trip early today, and I won't be expecting you out of bed until supper."

Inhaling deeply, Selina shook her head. "You've already done so much for me, and I'll never repay you if I take time off. Goodness, Mrs. Jessup, I wouldn't dare think of taking advantage of your kindness."

Squinting in the sun, Susannah glanced around them as they stepped up to the shop. But she paused, finding Wyatt Thomas standing just ahead of them. He'd stopped in mid-step, one hand on his jacket and the other on a small box from the general store. The young man was staring at them, and so she offered a wave. The movement caught his attention, and he came over.

Taking his hat off, Wyatt nodded. "Hello, Mrs. Jessup. How are you today?"

"Wonderful." She grinned. His timing was perfect. Turning to Selina, she was glad to see she was looking well enough. The scratches were fading, and the yellowing bruise around her eye was hardly noticeable. She was very pretty and Wyatt couldn't seem to keep his eyes off her. "Mr. Thomas, it's been too long. Selina, this is Wyatt Thomas. Mr. Thomas, this is Miss Selina Carlson, from Boston. She's a guest in my home and we're shopping."

He nodded as though the conversation were fascinating, his eyes focusing more on Selina than anything else. Wyatt fiddled with his hat in his hand and gave Selina his best smile. "How do you do, ma'am? It's a pleasure to meet you."

It really was too perfect. "Thank you, sir." Selina nodded demurely, keeping her gaze down. "The pleasure is all mine."

She was much more difficult to read but at least there would be time on the ride home to discuss this moment. Selina was doing a good job of being polite while holding Wyatt's interest.

The man took a deep breath, putting his hat back on and fiddling with the box with both hands. He shifted his weight three times and opened his mouth to say something before closing it again. It was clear how taken he was with Selina, and he was definitely curious. It seemed as though he didn't know what to do with himself. Susannah had seen the indecision and doubt time and time again, but knew what to do about it now.

"We're in a hurry, I'm afraid," she cut through the silence gently. "But Mr. Thomas, would you be so kind as to join us for supper tomorrow?"

"Oh, I couldn't be a bother." He shook his head.

To their surprise, Selina spoke up. "We'd love it if you'd join us."

Wyatt grinned from ear to ear. "All right, yes. Tomorrow, then. Thank you, ladies."

Susannah smiled and nodded. "Lovely. We'll see you then. Have a lovely day, Mr. Thomas."

He tipped his hat at them and turned to walk back down the street.

Susannah smiled but paused as she looked at Selina. Biting her lip, she tried to think back and decide if the girl knew the main purpose of the boarding house. Had they discussed finding a husband?

Surely she was here to find a husband. But the more she thought about Selina's first days, she was certain they'd not discussed matchmaking at all. Her heart grew heavy at the thought of another misunderstanding. Susannah bit her lip and furrowed her brow. She would have to have a conversation with Selina, and soon.

Chapter Eleven

It had only been three nights and four days. Selina was gone and Mary began to jump at every sound. Her actions had been rash, she knew, but also her only choice. Just thinking of her battered niece made her shudder all over again. And then she shuddered a second time at the thought of her husband finding out what she'd done to help her escape.

He came home drunk three nights in a row, unable to say anything intelligible enough for Mary to understand. She would bring him food and a mug of coffee and then prayed he would stay asleep. And for four days, James simply wasn't around. Working and gambling with friends, he often went through phases where Mary had much needed time to herself.

That's how it had been nearly twenty years ago, the night he beat her so badly she didn't need to go to a doctor to know she would never have children. James had left for over a week then and came home acting as though nothing had happened. She could walk again by then, and they never spoke of it. Because of that experience, Mary desperately hoped James would let it go about Selina. It would be best if he'd forget she had ever been there, but that wasn't going to happen.

After all, Ben had been with them longer. And James had merely seen him off on the day he left, and never mentioned him again, as if the young man had never existed. Surely, Mary prayed, the same would happen this time around. He couldn't have truly meant his crude actions towards the girl, and his being gone was his form of an apology.

She found out on the fourth night she was wrong. Her husband came home earlier than he had all week, whistling a jaunty tune as he came through the door. The man had once been handsome, she reflected, and wondered what had happened. She wasn't sure if he'd aged so poorly or if she'd learned to see him for the reprobate he was.

"Good evening," he chuckled, finding her staring at him with soap suds dripping off her hands and onto the floor. "Cleaning up the floor already? I thought you had another month before it was time." It wasn't exactly a joke, but he laughed all the same.

Mary glanced down and shrugged, putting her hands back in the sink. "No, you simply caught me by surprise." She offered a wan smile. "I didn't know you'd be home so soon. But I'm glad," she added hurriedly. "Now you can join me for supper."

He set down his toolbox and glanced at the table. She always set his place in case he was there in time. Mary's heart hammered, and she prayed today was a good one until finally he nodded his approval and took a seat. "It smells great. Come on over, then."

She eyed his dirty hands before nodding. Perhaps she'd worry about his filthy hands another time. Rubbing her hands dry on her apron, she crossed over and sat with him at the small round table. "I know how you enjoy a good hearty roast." And Mary passed him the bread.

After taking a huge bite, he put four thick slices on the plate leaving one for her. She put it on her plate and tried to think of something to say. "How was your day?" She paused, watching him cut into the meat on his plate. She swallowed. Things had been going well, and she dreaded saying the wrong thing.

The man groaned and talked about how annoying his superiors were. James had always believed he was meant to run the factory but had never managed to get further than working on the conveyor belt. She knew he worked hard, but also was aware that many could find his attitude too harsh.

Still, she nodded along and frowned at the right parts of his story. "I'm so sorry, dear. Hopefully they'll notice your hard efforts soon," she assured him. "They must."

But he just grunted and took a large bite of his roast. As he chewed, James looked around, squinting as if he needed to find just the right thing. Mary tried to follow his gaze, but couldn't.

"What is it, dear?" she attempted to ask in a light tone. "Is everything all right?"

James scowled. "Where's that girl? Selina? She always joins us for supper."

Her mouth went dry. All the lies and plans she'd cooked up disappeared from her mind. She couldn't remember a single part of her story since she'd hoped he'd let it go. What was she supposed to say? What had she been planning to say? "Oh, right. Selina. Our niece. Well, she isn't here tonight. She just isn't here. I thought it was nice to just be us. It's sweet to have supper like we used to." She thought focusing on something besides Selina might help him forget about her.

"When is she coming back?" His voice was low and almost angry.

The blood drained from her face as she knew he wasn't about to let this matter go. Not now, and not tomorrow. "I don't know, James, I'm sorry. Soon, I'm sure."

Her husband glared and then shot up from his seat. "I'm going to go look for her."

"What?" She rushed up. "Why would you do such a thing? I'm sure she's on her way back even now." But she couldn't stop him. James left the house and disappeared into the evening. Mary watched him go incredulously, wrapping her arms around her shaking body. What was he going to do when he came back and still couldn't find her?

Eventually Mary had the answer. It was two nights later when her lies ceased and she couldn't think of anything else to say. Demanding a better answer, James smacked Mary hard enough for her to fall on the table and she was certain she saw stars.

"Where is that girl?" James gritted his teeth and kicked her shin. Mary wondered if she was the only one who had heard the crack and started to collapse, but he grabbed her by the neck and pinned her against the wall. She gagged, pulling at his hands.

"P-please," she gasped.

But the man she had married only glared, a darkness in his gaze told her how little he cared for her. Mary's heart beat frantically as she tried to writhe away, but there was no escaping him now. "I wasn't finished with her," he hissed.

Mary coughed, unable to get enough oxygen. She blinked hard, feeling his grip only tighten. She was seeing stars again. "I—I don't… I can't breathe."

He released one hand to punch her in the ribs and Mary could hardly cry out. Tears filled her eyes and she couldn't see him clearly. Desperately she grabbed for his face and scratched it before he was able to move away. He punched her again and pinned her arms down with one hand, and his other still wrapped around her neck.

"Tell me, or I won't let go," he threatened her. "And I'll know if you're lying."

Mary's face crumpled, her strength fading with every second. After all she'd done for the girl, she wouldn't be able to save her. She knew that now. She had tried, and she would fail. "Co-Colorado," she sobbed.

"Where? Where in Colorado?"

"Rocky Ridge. But she—" He didn't care for anything more and slapped her so hard she blacked out.

Mary woke, gasping for breath. Her stomach heaved and her ribs ached. Rolling to her side, she looked up to see her neighbor's boy, Daniel, staring down at her. Behind him was his father, Mr. Dillard. He brought over a cold cloth and smiled tightly.

"What happened?" Her throat was as dry as the wastelands and voice cracked.

Her neighbor glanced apprehensively at the front door with a frown before turning back to her. "We heard a ruckus and saw your husband run out. Emily came to check on you and saw you on the floor. We came over and found you here, so she's gone for the doctor. He'll be here soon, so don't move."

She had been trying to sit up, but she was too shaky

and had to do what he said. They waited and finally Dr. Hathaway arrived.

"You're the one who brought Miss Carlson to us, aren't you?" he murmured and gently touched her neck.

Tears filled her eyes before she burst out into pitiful sobs. They shook her body as she curled into a ball, ashamed and terrified of what was to come next. Her neighbor, Emily, hugged her, and it took several minutes for Mary to gather herself to finally tell them what happened.

When she was finished with her story, they were quiet until the doctor straightened up. "Mr. Dillard, please find the sheriff immediately. We need to find James Robinson before someone else is hurt—or killed."

They searched for him for several days, but Mary knew he was gone. The man knew where to look for Selina now. She knew there was no way he was still in town. She only hoped that Selina had found support who would defend her by the time she saw James again.

Chapter Twelve

He stopped on the porch and double checked his appearance. His boots were polished and his trousers were clean. His shirt and vest were both pressed. Pulling off his hat, he ran a hand through his dark blonde hair and hoped it was short enough to look decent. He hadn't had it cut in some time and it almost brushed his shoulders.

Wyatt Thomas fixed his jacket and took a deep breath. If he could fight two men at once and race another through town all before breakfast, he could survive a supper with friends. And with Miss Carlson.

"Good evening." The door opened sooner than he'd anticipated. He was enchanted to see Miss Carlson was greeting him.

Snatching his hat off, he tried to smile, and nodded at her. "Evening," he responded immediately. "I—um, thank you. Yes. I'm not late, am I? Or too early?" She was wearing an apron, and ladies usually only wore them while they were still in the kitchen. That meant she was either still baking or cleaning up.

She tilted her head up in confusion and followed his gaze. "Oh." She realized, and hurriedly took it off.

"No, not at all. My apologies. Do come in. Might I take your hat?"

Wyatt glanced at his hat in confusion, wondering why she would want to take it. For a moment they stood there until his eyes caught sight of the coat rack. "Oh, to put on the…right. Yes, thank you." He relaxed and handed it over.

As Selina led him into the sitting room, he couldn't help but watch her. She walked with a sway, a loose movement that reminded him of a willow tree. And tonight she wore her hair down, and it trailed silkily down her back. It was like a soft dark brown waterfall, and Wyatt had to resist the urge to touch it.

"There you are!" Mrs. Jessup turned when they came into the room though her husband was already watching them. "Wonderful. Thank you, Selina. Now, if we're all ready, let's eat."

She beckoned for them to follow her to the table.

"I'm certainly ready to eat." Lucas smiled and followed his wife.

"Do sit down, please. Lucas, would you bring the pitcher?"

Wyatt and Selina sat as Lucas and Susannah came near. He pulled out his wife's chair for her, and Wyatt froze, watching the movement. Instantly he regretted not having thought of holding Miss Carlson's chair. He'd eaten at the Jessup's home before, but not for a fancy gathering like this and he was nervous. There were several dishes on the table, and everyone was dressed in some of their best clothes. Tonight was different, for he'd never shared a meal with such a pretty woman.

Glancing at the roast chicken, he picked up a fork but wasn't sure how to best proceed, so he waited to watch

Miss Carlson start. But when she didn't start eating, he realized she was waiting for him. The realization struck her at the same time and the young lady looked up in surprise. A sheepish grin crossed both their faces before they relented and carefully dug in.

"Mr. Thomas, how is your ranch these days?" Mrs. Jessup asked politely.

He paused and wiped his mouth as politely as he knew how. "Good." He glanced around the room. "I have some fat head of cattle to get me through the winter. And I just purchased two goats. I don't know what I'll do with them yet," he added sheepishly, "but I'll figure it out. I've heard they're right handy."

Selina didn't say anything, but Mrs. Jessup beamed. "That's lovely! Lucas, didn't Eleanor just purchase one? Didn't she? Was it for the milk?"

After a moment, the other man nodded. "Yes, dear, for the milk. Goats are good to have around, Wyatt. But you'll need to be careful. They can be right ornery."

For some reason, Mrs. Jessup suddenly gasped. Turning to her husband, she patted his arm. "Dear, you should tell your story. The one about the escaped goat? He was ornery, that one. Why, that was nearly seven years ago! Neither of you were here for it, you see, but Dr. Fitzgerald thought goat milk might be healthy. He had just arrived in town and hardly a soul knew him. After this happened, of course, everyone knew him. Lucas, tell them."

He grinned. "Are you certain you don't want to share it? I believe the story's just about told." She gave him a stern look, and Lucas chuckled. "As she said, Dr. Fitzgerald had just bought himself a goat. The problem here was they work better in sets, and it's easier to purchase them younger than older. He didn't know this, so he bought a single older goat. His first mistake was taking the goat to his office, and the second was not knowing how to milk her."

He felt the eyes on him, and Wyatt glanced at Selina who held his gaze curiously for a moment before dropping her eyes. Hiding a grin, he listened to Lucas telling about how the goat escaped through the back door and terrorized the pastor's wife by ripping half her skirts off.

Susannah covered her mouth. "I remember it like it was yesterday. Oh, the poor woman. No one saw her for nearly half a year. She couldn't bear to face people who'd seen her petticoats. But no one blamed her. She's the sweetest thing."

Chuckling, Lucas leaned back. "From the chaos, I thought we were in the middle of a shootout." He met Wyatt's gaze before turning away. Wyatt shrugged it off and pretended nothing happened though Susannah noticed the glance between them and started watching.

"I found all the boys around town tired from racing after the goat. She was grazing with the chickens as if nothing had happened by the time I found her!" Lucas chuckled.

Susannah clapped cheerfully. "Yes, that's true! Like nothing had happened! Everyone talked about it for months."

"What happened to the goat? After you caught her?" Selina asked, propping her chin up on her hand.

Scratching his head, Lucas shrugged. "When Dr. Fitzgerald came for her, he realized he had no idea what he was doing so he gave her away. I don't remember who. Susie darling?"

Everyone turned to Susannah. Chuckling, she bit her

lip with a thoughtful nod. "You won't believe this, but he gave it to the pastor and his wife!"

There were several more stories shared, and Wyatt had a few that would have matched Lucas's. But he knew his old ways weren't favorable and kept quiet, letting the Jessups do the talking. But then Lucas mentioned Luis the Sixer, and Wyatt started.

"Did you know about him?" Lucas noticed the movement.

Wyatt nodded, running a hand through his hair. "I sure did. Why do you ask?" He swallowed. "I mean, a little. Worked with him a bit."

"What did you do?" Selina asked him.

His throat went dry, and he tried to figure out how to best respond. To his surprise, Lucas saved him.

"He worked with the law. Honorable man here, Mr. Thomas. Basically, he was a traveling deputy. I'm sure you're quite skilled, to have worked with Luis."

"Thanks," Wyatt muttered dryly.

Susannah smiled uncertainly, not understanding what had just happened but definitely feeling the building tension. Sniffing, she stood up. "This has been splendid. How about we go for a walk, shall we? Let's go together since it's a lovely night."

Wyatt struggled to stay beside Selina once they started out. He wasn't used to being careful to think of a woman at his side. They walked slowly side by side. He looked ahead to Lucas taking Susannah in his arm and then glanced down at Selina and opened his mouth. He wanted to offer his arm but couldn't find the words. When he turned, the moonlight reflected on her pale face, emphasizing her features as well as the marks on her face.

He knew they were there. The scratches dripping down her chin and a faded black eye. Wyatt was a man who had given plenty of hurts as well having been on the receiving end before. He knew what a bruise looked like in all its colorful phases. Dropping his gaze, he walked with her and wondered what had happened.

Had it been an accident? It could have been a bad fall, or there were some animals who could inflict some serious bruising if she was attacked. But people could also do damage to others. Shaking his head, Wyatt sighed. People were capable of such cruelty. It still pained him to have been surrounded by such violence, and he was grateful to be away from the lifestyle. He'd been a young angry boy, thinking being part of the gang would solve all his problems. Now he knew better and was free of the rough life.

"Is everything all right?" Selina asked.

Wyatt offered a grim smile. He knew the pain she must have experienced, and it frustrated him no one had saved her from it. But Miss Carlson gave the appearance of wanting to keep some things private, and he understood that well.

"Everything is perfect," he told her softly. Wyatt stole another glance at her and tried to imagine wanting to be anywhere else with someone else. And he couldn't. "It's a lovely evening."

She nodded thoughtfully. "You're right. It is."

Selina wanted to tell him everything about herself, about her past, about every thought in her mind. The urge didn't go away, but the fearful side of Selina didn't allow her to say a single word.

Chapter Thirteen

Sundays were wonderful days in the Jessup household and the main event was the service at church. She'd never been there before, but she knew what it was. She'd longed to go, but knew she'd never be allowed as long as she lived with Aunt Mary and Uncle James.

The pastor at the Rocky Ridge church read from the Bible. It was a passage she knew because her cousin, Ben, had shared this one with her. It lifted her heart, and she suddenly felt blessed to be here. There was a family Bible in the sitting room in the Jessup house and she read that one every day.

When she'd unpacked her few belongings out of the bag Aunt Mary packed for her, the Bible was not there. She was disappointed to lose it, but she was also thankful she had a new place to live and a Bible was available to her. There was nothing like the energy and spirit she felt when she was in the House of God. And besides, Wyatt Thomas was there.

He started to join them at their bench on Sundays, and Susannah suggested Selina invite him over to lunch afterwards. He was quiet, but he began to tell her more about himself. It turned out he was a bright man who had read much, gone far, and done a great deal with his life already.

Sometimes she didn't have the energy for a stroll so they'd sit on the porch out in the sun, but Selina tried to save her strength so they could at least walk around the barn. With the sun warm on her face and Wyatt beside her, she was happy enjoying their conversations and even the silence.

He made her feel safe though she couldn't put her finger on why. The man was respectful and careful, all the while never doubting her strength or resolve. Selina had noticed how he avoided some topics of his own as well as never asking about her occasional limp or the fading marks on her skin.

All Wyatt ever had to give was a quick smile and friendship she clung to. She prayed he would continue to remind her men could be good. If so, that would be enough. And that's why she wanted to tell him. Selina wished Wyatt knew how much good he was doing, the courage he was restoring in her. But if she told him, then he would know everything.

He wouldn't see her the same, not if he knew the truth. To open her heart after all the pain and tragedy she had faced, Selina would just be asking for trouble.

"Are you all right?"

"Hmm?" Selina jumped at his touch, Wyatt's fingers brushed lightly against her elbow. "Oh, I'm sorry. I was daydreaming, I suppose. What did you say?"

Though his eyes were dark, they held not a single hint of malice or anger. If anything, only merriment. Wyatt ran a hand through his long hair and smiled.

"Just wondering what's on your mind. I know my stories aren't great, but I didn't know I was boring you."

She flushed though she knew he was joking. "I'm sorry. I didn't mean to ignore you." She took a deep breath and shook her head. "Wyatt, do you ever feel like there's a big knot you can't untie?" Rubbing her hands together, she looked down and took several steps before noticing he had stopped in his tracks.

As she looked back, he hastened to catch up to her. The merriment had faded. Selina didn't notice it at first, but on a second look at his face, she saw a shadow there. "I do." Wyatt nodded and shifted his weight. "That I do. Why do you ask me?"

Biting her lip, she glanced down at her hands again. The bandage on her wrist was gone, but it stilled ached often. Sighing softly, Selina shook her head. "What do you do about it?"

He brushed his hands against hers before stepping back and placing his hat back on his head. She didn't recoil at his touch, but waited anxiously to hear if he knew of a secret she didn't. "The only thing you can do, I'm afraid, is to find something very sharp and cut right through it."

She couldn't contain her laughter as she'd expected some wise piece of advice. She shook her head as he chuckled. The tension she hadn't realized was in the air was immediately gone and she relaxed. The evening went by far too fast and soon it was time for Wyatt to leave.

The following morning, Selina was still thinking about what he'd said. As much as she wanted to consider how it might apply to her, she couldn't get over his funny answer. It had been an amusing comment, but maybe there was more to it. Cutting away the knot instead of trying to untangle it might be a reasonable approach and she needed to think about how she could do it.

In the meantime, though, she was still laughing. What an idea! She snorted and shook her head.

"What's so funny?" Susannah glanced over, wiping her hand across her cheek leaving a smudge of dirt. Even with dirt on her face, she was a natural beauty. They were on their hands and knees, digging through the garden pulling weeds before the sun rose too high.

Not sure how to put it into words now, Selina just shook her head. "It's nothing, I'm sorry. I was simply thinking about something Mr. Thomas was telling me about yesterday. That's all." Even then, she couldn't resist a small smile. Grabbing two weeds, she pulled them from the soft soil and tossed them in the nearby bucket.

"So your Mr. Thomas is good company?" Susannah asked after a moment.

"I think so, yes." Selina nodded, and turned to one particularly hearty weed. It had been growing in a corner of the garden and had taken advantage of the sun and water to claim a firm hold.

Susannah chuckled. "What a relief, then. I was worried when you arrived, you see, because we never really broached the topic of the matchmaking. You weren't aware of what I do before you arrived. Coming out west alone is hard, I know. It's different here. While we haven't talked much about serious topics, I just wasn't sure what to tell you. And when Wyatt became my client, I wasn't sure who to match him with. Since you seem to be getting along so well, maybe that question has an answer." She looked up at Selina, her smile fading away.

But Selina didn't notice. She'd stopped weeding though she still held on to the stubborn weed. Suddenly, the air was too hot, and she felt faint. Her vision went blurry and her hands started to tremble. After two tries, she got to her feet.

"Selina?" Susannah asked her cautiously, but she didn't hear her.

Staggering, Selina clutched her chest as she gasped for air. "What?" She managed to squeak out finally. "What on Earth are you talking about? Wyatt's looking for a wife? He came to you for that?"

Susannah took her arm before she tipped over. Grabbing one of the girl's hands, she led her to the porch where she leaned against the steps. "I thought you knew," Susannah fumbled. "Things were progressing between you and Wyatt and I just let nature take its course. You're happier around him. And truthfully, I didn't set this up. Everything fell into place without my intervention."

Her eyes nearly bugged out, wondering if the woman was telling the truth. "So what? You decided you might as well marry me off since I'm the only girl in your boarding house right now?"

Susannah flipped her hair back and took a deep breath. "Please, Selina, that's not what happened at all. In all my advertising I'm clear about the purpose of the boarding house. I thought you knew. I was sure your aunt would have mentioned that when she sent you here."

She tried to think back to what Aunt Mary had told her, but in the heat of the moment nothing was coming to mind. Shaking her head, she gulped in a deep breath and staggered up the steps. Susannah tried to help, but she shook her off. "It doesn't matter to me who knew what or when. I can't do this."

Selina made it to the door though Susannah called after her. The fear hammered in her heart and she flinched as the other woman touched her shoulder. Shuddering, she brushed her away. How could she pretend to be kind when she pushed women into marriage?

"Please," Susannah asked plaintively, "Selina, let's talk about this a bit more. I can tell you more and then you'll understand."

"No." Selina shook her head sharply. "I won't be a man's prize again. I won't put myself in that position ever again."

Her throat closed up, and she marched inside, refusing to look back. Her body shook in anger and frustration, realizing everything she had here had been nothing as she had imagined.

Chapter Fourteen

It's not that bounty hunters were bad people, Lucas reflected thoughtfully, it was that they didn't work with the law. If anything, they acted like outlaws themselves, bringing in wanted criminals for the money. They did it for their own gain, and not for the sake of justice.

Wyatt Thomas strolled into town and headed into the general store. From his office, Lucas could watch the folks on the street. He strolled around every day through town making sure all was well. He had keen senses that picked up when something was amiss.

As Mr. Thomas disappeared, Lucas looked for something else to attract his attention. He thought about the man a bit as he stepped into the shade on Main Street. Granted, Wyatt Thomas wasn't a bad man. He was quiet but careful and clearly smart, not like some other bounty hunters he'd known in his lifetime. The young man had to be skilled if he had worked with Luis the Sixer who had the best reputation for success.

But it wasn't his business. Lucas shook his head, trying to clear his mind. Just because he was of a certain mind didn't mean he was always right. If he could leave the life of the rangers, others could as well. Wyatt showed no sign of restlessness or boredom, but had adjusted well.

Sure enough, Wyatt came out of the store with his arms filled with flour, sugar, and a few more items Lucas couldn't identify from this far away. Lucas thought back to his younger days. Shaking his head, he sighed and wondered how the time flew by so quickly. One day he was on his first job with the Rangers, and the next he had been married for ten years to the perfect woman.

After a few minutes of pacing on the sidewalk, he saw a familiar wagon drive down the street and around the corner. "Jeb—" he peeked his head in the office "—should I go get your mail?"

Jeb glanced up and nodded. "Yes, please."

Lucas headed out and about to check on things on the street. After catching a stray hoop for the rambunctious children, he rolled it back to them and talked with the pastor on his way. Afterwards, he reached the post office and requested all items for the Harbins, Jessups, and the sheriff's office. There were a few scattered items, and he whistled as he took everything back to his deputy.

"Here we are." He handed over a letter, and put one in his jacket. The letter he tucked away was from one of Susannah's aunts and he was sure his wife would be happy to get it. He grinned, just imagining his beaming wife dancing around the room. At least, she would as long as the letter was a happy one.

"Thank you," Jeb mumbled, hardly noticing. At his desk he sat with a biscuit in one hand and a pen in the other, trying to take care of the legal documents. That was the boring part of the job, but it had to be done.

Chuckling, Lucas shook his head. Better Jeb than himself. Running a hand through his hair, he returned to his own desk and started on the paperwork he was responsible for as sheriff. Turning to the filing cabinet, he sorted a few papers regarding arrests and incidents in the area.

He heard a groan and looked up to see Jeb stretching. "I'm going to get something more to eat. Do you want anything?"

Shrugging, Lucas shook his head. "No, not today."

Jeb nodded, pulling on his hat. "I'll be back soon."

Lucas turned to the last mail item, a packed file of recent wanted posters. Sometimes he wondered if the list grew every time and if it would ever end. But he knew the work of a lawman was never finished.

Humming, Lucas started to glance through them, trying to memorize the face sketches and the names. There were only three papers left when something caught his eye. Boston. Frowning, Lucas glanced at the script again. James Robinson, wanted in Boston for assault on women. The last part was just an emphasis on the law's desire to catch the man, and Lucas didn't blame them. Any man who hurt a woman was a coward and deserved to be treated as one.

Shaking his head, Lucas held onto that one as he grabbed a few pins from his desk. One by one, he picked a flyer and put it on the board. This time around, Lucas had eight new posters to post. He stepped back, clutching three old papers that didn't need to be up any longer.

That's when the children playing on the sidewalk came to see the new posters. They bumped into each other and yelled out as they all hurried over. Raising an eyebrow, he watched as they crowded around the new pictures, getting louder by the minute. He just hoped they couldn't read—there were details in those posters no child should ever know about.

"He's got an eyepatch!"

"I'm playing him next time, that one. I get to be him!"

"I want to be Sheriff Jessup!"

"What about me? I want to be Mr. Harbin!"

Lucas couldn't help but chuckle at their games. It had to be nice to be so young and innocent, to see the world as fun. Part of him wanted to scold them for acting so light about this, but they deserved the chance to have a happy childhood. They didn't know any better and that was actually good. Let them play Outlaw and Sheriff until it became real. He didn't get to experience it, but someone should.

"Wait a minute," a voice called out behind Lucas. Everyone turned to see Jeb walking up to the children with a goofy grin. "Then who am I going to play?"

Most of them burst into giggles. "You can be the horse!" One laughed so hard he fell on the ground. Jeb winked at Lucas and looked down at the fallen boy. Immediately two other children grabbed onto Jeb's legs, trying to keep him from going back to his desk to work.

"Two sheriffs!" One of the little girls screeched, and she wrapped herself around Lucas's leg as well, sitting on his boot. The men cried out dramatically, pretending to lose their balance as all the children cheered. With the twelve children on their hands, Rocky Ridge's lawmen had their afternoon filled up. Lucas briefly hoped nothing big happened because the children would make it difficult for them to hurry out if they were needed.

Finally the afternoon ended and Lucas started for home. He wasn't far out of town when he heard a familiar set of hoofbeats coming up behind him. Slowing down, he glanced back and saw his deputy headed in his direction. Confused, Lucas pulled his horse to a stop and waited patiently, an eyebrow raised.

"Hey." The man nodded breathlessly with a sheepish grin. "I nearly forgot something. Something happened when I went out at lunch time. I haven't got a clue if it's important or not and you might already know. I thought it best to tell you straight away."

Impatient with Jeb's preamble, Lucas shrugged. "Out with it, Jeb. I don't have all day."

"Sorry, Sheriff. Anyway, someone was asking about your wife's guest. Leastways, I'm pretty certain it was about her. Overheard him in the mercantile but by the time I connected the dots, he was gone. I checked with the cook the man had been talking to. Someone from back East asking to see if a very pretty woman had come through town in the last month."

"Hmm. Interesting. Anything else?"

"The stranger didn't have a picture to show, and the cook wasn't certain about your boarding house girls so he said nothing. But good or ill, I wanted to let you know. In case you didn't already."

Thinking about it, Lucas slowly shook his head. "I didn't. But thank you, Jeb. I'll talk to Susie about this." The men parted and Lucas considered it as he headed home.

Coming from the garden, Susannah waved and was ready with a kiss by the time he entered the kitchen.

"It's about time you made it home," she commented with a grin. "Just in time to help me finish my cornbread. Tonight, it's just you and me. Selina was exhausted, so she just retired for the evening."

Jeb's words faded away, and he pushed it to the back of his mind. Lucas kissed her cheek. "I'm not complaining." He could talk to Selina later. Perhaps tomorrow. There were nicer things to focus on right now, like eating his wife's cornbread and telling her about the children in town and their games.

Chapter Fifteen

A full night's rest did her a world of good and Selina woke up just before the sun. There were no night horrors, just a darkness that helped her get the rest she had desperately needed. Not only did she feel awake and refreshed, but her mind was clear and she knew what she needed to do. Though her time here had been lovely, several things needed to be straightened out.

Once she'd brushed her hair thoroughly and dressed for the day, Selina pulled on her boots and made her way to the kitchen. There were mixed emotions as she found Susannah already up, humming quietly as she mixed what smelled like berry muffins. While she wasn't quite ready to speak with her, she would feel better if she actually requested permission before taking anything that didn't belong to her.

First, she cleared her throat. "Good morning," Selina offered politely, clasping her hands behind her back as she waited for Susannah to acknowledge her.

The humming died away as Susannah sighed, attempting a shy smile as she turned around. They hadn't spoken since yesterday in the garden. The tension was still there, and it only made Selina more anxious and she couldn't meet Susannah's gaze. "Is there any chance I might borrow the cart? I'd like to go into town." She spoke hurriedly before Mrs. Jessup could get a word in.

Susannah debated this for a moment in her mind before finally offering a nod. "I suppose so, yes. Is something wrong? I could come with you if you need me to. I'd hate to worry about you being alone, and you're only just now feeling better. Where do you need to go? I can—"

Susannah stood up and Selina waved a hand to stop her. "No, but thank you. I should return before noon to help prepare supper." She bit her tongue and considered mentioning her desire to discuss what had happened between them the day before. But now wasn't the time. Worrying about it would distract her from her first errand of the day.

"At least might I help you set up the cart?"

Her voice was meek and soft, almost enough to convince Selina to accept the suggestion, but she shook her head after thinking about it for a minute. It was a lovely day, and it would help her stretch her muscles by taking care of it herself. "Thank you, but no. I'll return when I'm able." After hesitating one last time, she offered a tight smile and made her way out the door.

Mr. Jessup had showed her how to strap the horse in and set the cart up for a journey. Fortunately she had a good memory and was able to get ready to go with little hassle before climbing into the seat.

At least the sun was out, she tried to tell herself. A nice day to get things done and to get her life in order. She owed herself that much as well as the others. She clenched the reins tightly and squinted at the road ahead. The ride was a short one, shorter as she focused on what she wanted to say.

Wyatt Thomas had told her about his ranch, nestled into the corner of a nice valley and had even told her how to get there. It was simple enough in this big sprawl of the country, for it was just off the beaten path before she reached town. Selina's memory served her well as she took a deep breath and headed onto his trail from the main road.

It was a long path up to the house, and her heart started beating much faster the moment she saw it. It was a lovely little place and its charm surprised her. Though she'd never seen Wyatt's home, his touch was clear. The house was quaint and newly finished.

As she drew near, she saw Wyatt stepping out of the house, putting his hat on. He was already dressed and ready to go for the day, acting almost as though he had expected her.

"Good morning," he called, coming out to meet her with the horse and cart. Tipping his hat, Wyatt patted the horse before helping her down. She accepted his hand reluctantly, glancing up at the man as she tried to keep her resolve. It was almost too easy to forget her troubles when he smiled so brightly at her.

Wyatt's dark eyes sparkled, and she wondered again how all of this was possible. As much as she had wanted to confide in him for the last few weeks, now Selina had to come about something else. Because he wasn't who she thought he was. His smile was a lie, and he was trying to deceive her. Such an idea made her ill, and she had to look away.

"Good morning," she managed hesitantly, trying to

decide how to dive into the matter. "Mr. Thomas, I need to speak to you. About something quite important."

Nodding, he stepped back and flashed her a grin she couldn't return. "Please, call me Wyatt. We've known each other long enough. Do you want to come into the shade to speak?"

Unconsciously she took a step forward, ready to accept, but it was a step in the wrong direction so she hurriedly backed up against the cart and shook her head. "Actually, I, um, Mr. Thomas, I would rather not." Selina swallowed and dropped her gaze. Tension built between them as she refused to use his first name. He noticed and his smile tightened as a crease built in his brow.

"Of course." He nodded politely and hesitated. "What can I do for you today, Miss Carlson?"

He was polite, but it came off more coldly than he'd ever spoken to her before. While she was certain he didn't mean it so harsh, it brought tears to the corners of her eyes. Holding her head high, Selina tried to hold herself up straight as she cleared her throat.

"I came to Rocky Ridge to escape the life I had in Boston. While I wholly intended to start over, I never had marriage in mind. I have recently learned you are a client of Susannah Jessup's matchmaking service and I believe I have been used unjustly."

There was a moment's delay as he frowned. "What?"

She forged ahead, trying to remember everything she wanted to say. The man moved and put out an arm to her, but she stepped aside smoothly. "I don't know what gave you the impression I was in the market for a husband, but I am not. And you have been lying to me. I won't have it. I won't," she added stubbornly, and paused breathlessly while she tried to finish her thoughts. Swallowing hard, Selina realized her palms were sweaty, so she rubbed them dry.

"What are you talking about?" Wyatt shook his head, but didn't try to move any closer. "I mean, it's true I went to Mrs. Jessup about her matchmaking abilities, but I hope you'll believe me, my intentions were good. When she suggested I start visiting, I was under the impression you knew about the service. I thought you were happy about seeing me. In truth, I forgot about her matchmaking because I liked you right away."

She shook her head impatiently and gave him a hard look. "Then why didn't you say something? Why did you just assume we were courting? Or close to it?" she added hurriedly, refusing to accept the fact that they had been courting. No one could start a courtship without an official request, could they?

He flushed as he brushed his hair out of his face. Desperately he looked for an answer in the air before throwing his hands up in frustration. "I didn't know it had to be said! Selina, please, I never meant to hurt you. I wouldn't ever knowingly do anything to upset you. Did we not enjoy each other's company?"

"That's beside the point," she groaned in frustration. Her hands formed fists and a stray tear escaped that she brushed away angrily hoping he didn't notice. "The foundation of our friendship was based on a lie. I won't fall for your deceptive practices."

He hesitated. "Deceptive practices?"

She stomped her foot. "You know what I mean, Wyatt. You're not dumb. At least, I didn't think you were. Until I found out about your lie. What else have you simply decided not to tell me?"

Wyatt rubbed a hand down his face. "I would have wanted to court you even if I'd met you without Mrs. Jessup. And the truth is, she didn't actually set up our meeting."

But Selina shook her head. "And now you tell me more lies? I cannot trust you, Mr. Thomas. I simply came to tell you we should stop seeing each other, and I'd rather not meet with you again. If you are a gentleman, you'll respect my wishes." The words came out more bitter than she intended, and tension hung in the air. Pursing her lips, Selina turned away. "Good day, Mr. Thomas."

Stunned, Wyatt stood there as she clumsily climbed back into the cart without his assistance, and drove away. She headed down the trail, clinging to the reins tightly. By then, her resolve was at its end and the tears broke free. Sniffling, she tried to clear her vision and headed back to the boarding house.

Chapter Sixteen

Selina Carlson was nearly out of sight by the time Wyatt finally closed his mouth. Swallowing, he blinked and squinted, seeing Selina growing smaller as she travelled away from him. Several minutes had passed since she left him. He could feel his mind still trying to catch up to what had happened. It felt like he had been thrown off a speeding horse, the air escaping his lungs and his body braced for impact.

He didn't know what to do. He hadn't known how to defend himself, having not expected her visit or her argument. Staggering to his porch, Wyatt wiped his brow and took a deep breath. Her harsh words rolled over him as he tried to understand.

Things had been going well. He'd been happy, and he thought she was, too. Actually, he was sure she'd been happy. It had been obvious in all their time together. Several times he'd considered asking her if he might court her, but he thought it best to spend a little more time together first. There was less pressure and as she said, a gentleman wouldn't presume things.

Maybe he should have mentioned the matchmak-

ing, he mused, and began to pace. Since she was staying with the Jessups, from the hints Susannah shared,
Wyatt had honestly believed Selina Carlson had come to
Colorado to marry. Wasn't that what all women wanted?
Granted, he didn't know much about women, but he'd
heard women needed husbands. Clearly, there was still
too much he didn't understand about women.

"What can I do about this?" Pacing, Wyatt muttered
under his breath while he tried to think of solutions. But
he'd never been in a situation like this one before and he
was stumped. Usually he could take a physical action
and handle any problem with brute force. But this was
something else. Another person, a wonderful person,
was struggling because of this mess. Because of him.

Her voice rang in his head. *I cannot trust you, Mr.
Thomas.*

When she'd said those words, Wyatt's heart stopped.
Then she wondered out loud about other lies. She
seemed certain he'd withheld details from her and she
was right. While he'd shared a few stories about his
life, there was much he'd left out. He'd told her about
losing his parents to a murdering bandit when he was
eleven. But he'd faltered when he tried to tell her how
that horrible experience had eventually molded his decision to become a bounty hunter.

She wasn't aware that he was a man with a tendency
to step outside the law to do his job. Correction—his
former job. In that life, he'd not been the gentleman he
wanted to be now.

Throwing his hat down, Wyatt turned back and
watched the dust in the air swirl closer to the road.
Upon seeing it, his first instinct was still to sniff the
wind, studying the direction of the horses. Automati-

cally his guard was up and he was scouting out the best angles and ready to evade the sunlight. It was a hard habit to break even as he rubbed his forehead and knew she was most likely headed back to the Jessups'. She wouldn't be coming back to see him. She'd said she was done with him and he believed her.

Starting fresh was difficult. He'd lost everything once, and he'd run away from the pain. Joining Luis the Sixer had changed him into a man who took control of everything at the expense of his integrity. It was supposed to have been easy this time around, to clean up and settle down while making something better of his life. By simply deciding to do it, he'd thought it could happen with hard work and determination like before.

"It should have been easier," he grumbled to himself and kicked the hat. It flew up in the air before dropping back down with a soft thump. It brought back memories, watching men rise and fall.

He accepted the way things had been but didn't want to continue down the same path. He wasn't sure why he couldn't tell Selina about that part of his past. There had been plenty of opportunities to tell her, but he'd ignored every one. His past wasn't his future, so why was he so uncertain?

What would happen if she found out the sordid details of what he'd done before he came to Rocky Ridge? If he told her how many times he'd used his guns, of the hard things he had done to get what he needed, he was sure she'd reject him. He laughed bitterly when he reminded himself that none of that mattered now since she'd discarded him without ever knowing about his history as a bounty hunter.

His thoughts momentarily spread broader. He didn't

want anyone to know. Nobody would accept him and that's the reason he'd hidden it. Knowing he could head into a sour bout of self pity, he tried to redirect his thoughts. Worrying over what may never happen wasn't helpful.

Picking up the hat, he shook his head and frowned at it. Biting his lip, he headed towards the steps of the house again, when a memory came to mind.

Just two weeks ago, they'd taken a stroll after church. He had promised Mrs. Jessup he'd return Selina back to the boarding house safely. It was a nice day out and Selina had fixed her bonnet as she glanced up at him curiously.

"I don't know much about you." Selina had tilted her head and jutted her chin out. Then she'd smiled. "Tell me something about yourself, Mr. Thomas."

At her intense gaze, he'd shifted on his feet unsure of what she wanted to gather from him. His mind went blank of everything he knew, so he shrugged. "Sure, but what do you want to know?"

She lowered her head, but he saw the beginnings of a smile. The cut on her lip was much improved, and only a dark line that stretched upward almost like a dimple remained. For a moment he watched her curiously as she finally said something more to guide him in the right direction. "Anything. What were your parents like?"

He kept the memories of his parents on a shelf in his mind as though it were a book he kept out as a reminder but tried not to open frequently. As the two of them walked around the outskirts of the Sunday crowd, Wyatt thoughtfully considered the scars of the past and how he might answer her question. Swallowing the lump in his throat, he decided where to begin.

"They were robbed one evening in town. It was summer, and a Saturday. I'd stayed out late to play in the alleyways. As I came home, two men raced from our yard and knocked me down. I went in to find my parents where they had been left by their killers. They'd been sitting by the window reading. The books had fallen from their hands to the floor."

"I'm so sorry, Mr. Thomas. You were young?"

"Yes, just a boy. We never had much, but my father was a printer and we would read every night. He always had books for us to read. That was important to him. I didn't appreciate it at the time, but I do now for sure."

"I suppose so. Tell me what they were like. I'd love to learn about them."

"My father's voice was like a summer wind. If that even makes sense. He spoke with confidence in deep even tones." He could feel her gaze on him so he tried to be as descriptive as possible. "They would take turns reading out loud. He'd tell me about the histories, and she'd tell me the stories. I worked in my father's shop and never went to school because I had all the learning I needed with them. And my mother, she whispered like a songbird. The ones that come out in early spring to remind you the weather is warming. Oh my folks, they loved their books, and I buried several with them."

She was quiet before finally resting a hand on his arm. Wyatt had tensed up on instinct, but forced himself not to move. "They sound like they were lovely people. I think I would have liked them very much," she said softly. "Thank you for telling me about them. You know, I lost my parents when I was a child as well, and I don't remember them much. It makes me sad that so little remains in my memory about them. In fact, I feel somewhat guilty about it."

"You shouldn't feel guilty about that, Miss Carlson. You were too young to remember everything. It's only natural that time would fade their memory."

"It's strange, isn't it? People come and go throughout our lives, but it's still up to us to become who we're meant to be. To find God's purpose in our lives."

As they completed their turn about the street, he guided her towards his cart. "What do you mean?"

Selina accepted his hand to help her onto the bench. "Even without their strong influence on you growing up after that day, you were able to become a good man. It's a hard thing, growing up and deciding who you're going to be. Deciding how to hear God's voice and what it means. But we all have to do it on our own."

Selina was right. It's a choice. Wyatt nodded, staring up at his house. It was a good, sturdy home ready for anything. But was he? Gritting his teeth, his heart pounded, and he came to the realization right then that he was a decent man. He'd changed his life, and he was choosing daily to follow the plan he believed God had for him. Yes, every day he tried to do better than the day before.

Selina was pushing him from her life. She'd not minced words about her intentions regarding that. But he wanted to clear the air with her once and for all. It may not change her mind, but that wasn't his true purpose. He simply wanted to do the right thing and be honest. If it softened her heart he'd be happy about it. If not, he'd understand and let her go.

He dusted off his hat and went to the corral. Resolve and determination helped him start the journey.

Chapter Seventeen

Once she was out of view from Wyatt Thomas's property, Selina had to slow the horse down as she attempted to rein in her nerves. Clucking her tongue, she took a deep breath and tried to force her hands to stop shaking. Wyatt's handsome face kept returning to her mind, his blustering words and poor excuses. As much as she wanted to believe his words, she just couldn't.

Thoughts like these kept her so preoccupied she didn't notice the man on horseback until she was blocked off from her path. On the last couple of blocks of Rocky Ridge, she'd taken a detour through a corner of town and suddenly couldn't move forward. At first, she didn't realize who it was, and opened her mouth to ask if he might move out of her way.

His appearance had drastically changed. Haggard, he had lost a lot of weight and now wore clothes too big for him. The cuffs kept his shirt from falling over his hands, but everything looked all wrong. His eyes drooped but his lips were pressed in a familiar hard line. And those eyes, the dark eyes that made her heart drop to the depths of her stomach, had nothing but pure hatred within them. Her mouth hung open in shock.

"It's about time you were out alone," he growled, jumping awkwardly off his horse.

James Robinson had never ridden a horse before leaving Boston and staggered before regaining his balance. He was getting used to it, but it still took him a few moments. But it was too late by the time Selina realized that had been her chance to run. Clutching the reins, she could only hear the blood rushing in her ears.

Was she really seeing him? Swallowing, she tried to remember how to breathe. For a moment she recalled the night horrors she'd experienced as a child, but they were nothing compared to this. The man was her nightmares come to life in the worst way. How had he found her? Feeling nauseated, Selina was too stunned to do anything but stare at him.

But he didn't have time for her confusion and pulled a gun out. "Get out!" She jumped at the sight of the revolver he suddenly began waving around in the other hand. "Down, now! Senseless girl, you thought you could run from me? Is that it? You thought I'd just let you go?"

Selina stumbled down, one hand on the cart. Her gaze dropped out to the open street beside them. He had stopped her taking a shortcut through a backstreet on the edge of town but it was nestled right beside a busy one. Ready to scream, she opened her mouth, but that's when James's hand covered it.

"Oh!" She yelped, jerking back, but he gripped her chin hard.

She began to panic as her frightening past flooded back. Frantically, Selina tried to free herself. Forgetting about the gun, she managed to pull his hand from her face and gathered her courage to move. Heart pounding, Selina raced towards the open streets as she gasped for air to call for help.

James snatched her back, yanking on her braid. Immediately she was pulled off her feet. Yelping, Selina fell back and never had a chance to even try to catch her fall. She hit the ground hard and gasped haggardly at the open sky, feeling her fingers clawing into the mud.

Move, she told her body, begging it to do anything. James muttered angrily as he towered over her, and she stared into the barrel of his gun. Selina wanted to cough but was too afraid to move, not knowing whether to look at her cruel uncle or his weapon.

"Get up," he demanded, grabbing her. Scrambling, she attempted to evade his grasp, but he looped a long arm around her so she staggered and stumbled as he pulled her away from the crowd. Further down the empty street they went, no one noticing what was happening.

Blinking hard, Selina desperately looked around for anything that might help her for she knew what would happen if he had his way. James had already tried to accost her and clearly didn't believe he had done enough. Trying to force back the tears, she tried not to think of the last time she had seen him as she tried to find an escape. Surely there was something she could do to get out of here.

When she tripped, Selina allowed her entire body to collapse. She became dead weight, hoping he would let go of her. The motion caught him by surprise and he wasn't prepared, so he let go to keep his balance. "Filthy girl, get back up and—"

Before he could grab her again, she rolled away and tried to turn around.

"Help! Oh, please help me!" She started yelling as loud as she could, turning towards the street. Selina had the slightest hope his gun wasn't loaded, or at least she hoped he wouldn't use it to avoid the noise. The last thing he needed was to attract attention.

But then he pulled the trigger, and a loud bang rang through the air. She froze. Had she felt something whip by her ear? For a moment she was thankful she wasn't hit and then panic took over again. Breathless, Selina couldn't move or clear her head. She was terrified as he dragged her back towards his horse.

Then her mind cleared, and she knew she had to fight for her life and her freedom. "I'm not going back," she whimpered and her voice wasn't as strong as she'd tried to make it. She kept talking and her voice became more confident and resolute. "Please, let me go. Uncle, please, don't do this. Don't do this, please!" Digging her feet into the ground, Selina's body shook as she tried to keep her wits about her, trying anything she could think of to not be taken back with him.

He hit her with the handle of his pistol. It caught her chin and knocked her off her feet. James kicked her hip when she started to get up, and she cried out for it was the same hip he had badly bruised just ten weeks before that hadn't quite healed yet. She tried to dodge another kick and caught the tip of his boot.

The man muttered under his breath and looked completely undone, terrifying Selina more than ever. Back in Boston, James had been a man who had wanted to take advantage of an opportunity. But now, he had deliberately gone out of his way to get her. The effort he had gone through made her wonder what he had in mind, but she couldn't worry about that now. She had to save herself from him no matter what his plan was.

He got on his knees beside her and leaned in close. His breath was sour and putrid as he breathed into her face. Unshaven with grimy hands, James was filthy. Clearly he hadn't bathed in weeks. His disgusting odor was so strong she gagged, trying not to heave.

"You think you can just run out on me, huh? On us? I guess you thought precious Mary would protect you." He hissed the words out angrily, then he laughed bitterly. "That little traitor got what she deserved, she sure did. She's a liar and a cheat, but you're worse than that. Yeah, girl, you're much worse. You know what you are, huh? You're nothing. Garbage. You were so lucky to be in my household but you betrayed me. You don't get to leave me until I say so, do you understand? You ugly good for nothin' traitor."

He was leaning on her now, his weight was crushing her. She screamed in terror and pain before he covered her mouth. Tears of frustration spilled down her cheeks and over his hands. Shaking, she tried to breathe but his hands were big and his smell was making her ill. Dizzy, Selina was about to give up the fight when James suddenly jerked away.

She inhaled deeply, wondering why he had suddenly disappeared. Lying there in the dirt, Selina stared up, wondering why the day looked so lovely when everything was going so wrong, Coughing, Selina forced herself to focus and work past the nerves. Anxiously she turned and managed to pull herself up.

As she came to her senses, she heard a scuffle and looked around at two men fighting. James punched the other man hard, and he fell to the ground. They'd moved into the shadows and she could only make out James and couldn't tell who the second man was or exactly what was happening.

Her heart was still racing, and she had her wits about her again, but she was weak and in pain. Her hip ached terribly and Selina was worried she couldn't walk. Much of her leg had gone numb, and she tasted blood.

Just as she was trying to get up to get a better view of the fight, a shot rang out. She froze, eyes wide, and she turned just as a second shot followed. Both figures collapsed. Her fingers grasped her skirts, waiting anxiously. But she heard nothing in the alleyway except her own beating heart. Swallowing hard, she forced herself up and looked around.

Her horse and cart were at the end of the alleyway. Surprised it was still there, she turned to go to it. She had to get out while she still could. Taking short limping steps, she started her escape.

Something seemed off, though, and she stopped. She looked back, half expecting James to be up and ready to pounce on her. Her dreams and her reality had been filled with that very scene and she knew it was a possibility. Taking a deep breath, she put her hand to her throat and stared at James. His figure was bigger, and she could see he was the one lying closest to her.

He might have been her uncle, but he was not a good man and had certainly never treated her as family— that was the kindest way to describe him. At the sight of him, Selina shuddered. She couldn't move for a good minute until she realized he wasn't moving. His eyes were glassy, and his chest was bloody.

The comfort was short-lived as she leaned back

against the wall, relieved he couldn't hurt her again. He couldn't hurt anyone ever again. But the relief faded when she noticed familiar a hat in the dirt and clasped a hand over her mouth. It was a little battered since the last time she had seen it that very morning, but she would have recognized it anywhere as Wyatt's favorite hat.

Her blood ran cold.

Chapter Eighteen

The kitchen had suddenly grown much warmer, and she felt faint. "What?" Susannah screeched as Lucas finished laying out the details. The blood drained from her face as his words sunk in and she shook her head. Flushed, she waved a hand around her face as she took a deep breath, trying to remain calm. The initial panic faded as he explained everything.

Her husband reminded her there was nothing she could have done. It seemed so unbelievable, but she forced herself to focus as she thought of Selina, wondering how she was doing. To have endured all the terrible things she'd faced before she got here and to have to go through it all over again was unthinkable. While clearly the young woman was strong, she had no idea how strong until now.

Susannah had never been able to find out what happened to Selina in Boston. The little Lucas had learned before returning home wasn't enough to answer all her questions, but it was enough to fill in the largest gaps.

"Susie darling?"

He wrapped his arms around her, burying her in his

embrace. But then all she could think about was how Selina hadn't had such comfort, and the thought made her sad. Wiping away a tear, she pulled away and shook her head.

"We have to get to her. Now. I can't believe she went through all this and she never told us. And now this has happened. She needs people who care about her. We need to see her. Perhaps she's hungry." Susannah turned and started putting together a basket with bread, butter, and jam. She added dried beef and a jar of sweet pickles. "Did she look all right when you saw her? How was she? Does she need a shawl?"

"She's going to be fine. She'll spend at least tonight in the doctor's office. But I think she'd like to see you." Bringing her shawl, he calmly wrapped it around her shoulders and picked up the basket of food. She clutched his arm as he steered her towards the front door.

Susannah's heart raced the whole trip into town. It seemed especially long today. She didn't speak for the whole journey, her mind on Selina and what she would say to help her.

Parking the cart, Lucas helped her down to the ground as she clutched a blanket and the food basket. Glancing up at Dr. Fitzgerald's office, Susannah anxiously hurried to the door and marched right in, unable to take it any longer. Lucas hurried after her, supporting her always.

She went through the main door to the hallway. Looking up and down, she was uncertain of which one was Selina's. There were five options. "I don't know which door to try. Lucas, which one is her room?" She had hardly finished the question when the doctor's wife came out of one room and came towards them.

Alice Fitzgerald was carrying several towels and bandages. Nodding, she offered a tight smile and motioned for them to follow her. She opened the door for them.

Then Dr. Fitzgerald looked up and smiled. "Well, well! Good to see you, good to see you. I'm certain Miss Selina will enjoy some company. Step inside, there's plenty of room for all of us."

He was wrong—there wasn't plenty of room. Lucas stood back in the doorway as Susannah stepped in. Lying on the cot against the wall, Selina slowly opened her eyes and looked at them. The right side of her jaw was discolored already, and she was still covered in mud. Besides the shaking hands, she looked better than Susannah had expected and she sighed in relief. She thought there would be much more blood.

"Oh, I'm so glad you're all right," Susannah breathed, and sat on the edge of the cot. "When I heard about it all I couldn't believe it. And, well, I'm horrified." She shook her head. "How are you feeling?"

Mrs. Fitzgerald helped Selina sit up, stuffing an extra pillow behind her for support. The girl paled but managed to draw a deep breath as she glanced around the room. "I'll be all right," she rasped finally. "You didn't need to come."

Waving her hand, Susannah frowned. "Nonsense. You need support and no matter what, we're here for you. Selina, we care for you. Oh, I brought you your shawl. It gets cold at night and since you're staying here, I thought you might like it. When I return tomorrow, I'll bring some clean clothes."

It took a minute, but finally Selina nodded, managing a half smile. But the smile quickly disappeared as she winced and touched her jaw. Mrs. Fitzgerald dipped a cloth in a basin of water and pressed it against Selina's cheek. "You shouldn't talk," the woman murmured quietly.

Nodding, Dr. Fitzgerald peered at Selina over his wife. "Indeed, indeed. Let's see here. That's quite the jaw you have there, Miss Carlson. A fine, sturdy one and fortunate it's not broken. The bruise might last a while. How are your teeth? Did any fall out? No? Well, more good news there." He went through his check up and added a fourth pillow to the cot to help with her injured hip. Unless there was blood or anything definite broken, there wasn't much he could do.

Susannah and Lucas stayed there until the doctor finished. He explained the situation to the Jessups and Selina fell asleep before they left the room. "She'll heal fairly quickly, I believe. No internal injuries." Dr. Fitzgerald assured them again as they closed the door behind them to let her rest. "After a few days, she should be able to make it back to your house where I think she'll be much more comfortable."

Susannah and Lucas looked at each other and nodded as Dr. Fitzgerald continued.

"Most of her injuries aren't serious, though I'm concerned about her hip. This will take a few months to heal. She'll have pain for a while as she moves around, but staying active will help. It's possible this injury might affect her for quite some time."

Susannah blinked. "Are you saying she might be crippled?"

With a sigh, Dr. Fitzgerald's cheerful expression faded away and Susannah's heart beat anxiously in her chest. "I don't know how bad the injury is yet, and it'll take a good day or two to know for certain. I don't think she'll be able to garden for a while. Otherwise, she is a very strong young woman and I'm hopeful for a complete recovery."

Nodding, Susannah turned to her husband. "I'm staying here tonight. I don't care if she sleeps the entire time, but I don't want her alone. I'll be here if she needs me."

"The man who attacked her is dead," Lucas pointed out with a creased brow. "And you need your rest. I think you should just come home with me and we'll be back early tomorrow."

Shrugging, Susannah offered a tight smile. "Dr. Fitzgerald, if you don't mind, I'd like to spend the evening in Selina's room. I won't be a problem. I'll just take the chair. Lucas, you know I rarely get enough sleep and I'll be sure to get to bed early tomorrow if you want to be so particular. But Selina will not be alone if I have anything to say about it."

The firmness was set in her tone, and Lucas sighed. "Fine. Dr. Fitzgerald, we'll return in a short while, if that's all right by you?"

The doctor shrugged. "Whatever you like, Sheriff. The ladies would be safe enough either way, but it's up to you. If you don't mind, I'm going to check on my other patients. Let me know if there's anything else I can do to help." He tipped an imaginary hat with a wink and turned down the hall.

"Are you sure, Susannah?" Lucas asked once they were alone. Wrapping an arm around her waist, he led the two of them outside and down the street. "You don't have any reason to feel responsible and nothing will happen to her tonight. Her attacker is dead."

Susannah shook her head. "I want to stay."

He kissed her forehead. "All right." Leaving the matter there, he took her back to his office where he sent word to the Boston authorities that James Robinson was dead. Susannah thought of what she could piece together of Selina's difficult past as she settled down in her room. Not far away, Lucas took a seat out front, just within earshot.

Selina slept restlessly, moving often and groaning at the pain. Susannah dozed, jumping awake each time Selina shifted. "No!" The young girl called out just before dawn. Sweat drenched her forehead, and she shivered as she attempted to get up. Susannah grabbed her by the shoulders and the girl struggled weakly against her. "Stop it, please, let go!"

"Shh," Susannah whispered, touching the girl's face tenderly. "Selina, you're safe. Shh, now. You're safe, and everything's all right." Standing over the girl, she draped the damp cloth back on Selina's forehead as she panted, looking around in the darkness. "You're at the doctor's, Selina, do you remember?"

The door creaked open. "Susannah?" Lucas asked quietly.

She waved a hand behind her. "We're fine, it's all right. Selina? You're safe, I promise. It's Susannah. You're doing just fine."

Her own heartbeat began to slow back down as the girl winced and reluctantly slipped back down onto the cot. Already her eyelids were drooping and within minutes, she was asleep again. Susannah settled back into the chair and prayed for healing and comfort for Selina. Hopefully the long night was nearly over and new hope would come with the rising sun.

Chapter Nineteen

Although everyone had hoped Selina would be well enough to return to her own bed the following day, Selina didn't have the strength to even sit up. Clearly, she needed more time to heal before she could travel to the Jessup home. She spent her time lying down and staring at the ceiling, trying not to think.

There was a knock on her door two days later, and she rubbed her eyes. "Come in." She was expecting to find Susannah there since the woman was visiting her daily. It was frustrating since Selina was still upset with her, but Susannah had told her they would talk about their concerns once she was feeling better. And she was too tired to ignore or push away.

But it was Mr. Jessup. He ducked his head in with an apprehensive smile. Hesitantly, he stepped into the doorway. Glancing around, he surveyed the room for a minute before turning to her. The motion made her think of Wyatt Thomas who did this upon entering any new space. She could see the closed door across from Lucas; he supposedly was resting. She wondered quickly how he was doing, but put her mind back to Lucas Jessup since he was standing in her room.

"I'm sorry, I missed what you said," she managed vaguely when Lucas spoke.

"It's all right." He smiled and held up two pieces of paper. "Here you are, Miss Carlson. The first is a telegram from your aunt, arrived here this morning. And I received this from Boston. They'll be closing the files on your uncle, Mr. James Robinson."

Selina looked at him with a blank expression. She wasn't sure what to think.

"Apparently he caused trouble between Boston and here as he travelled, so they set out a reward. Three hundred dollars. Enough to take you wherever you'd like. Susie mentioned you were considering leaving, and I wanted to let you know I can write back immediately and request the funds delivered to you here while you recuperate."

She frowned and glanced at her hands. Lately, she just couldn't make the shaking stop. So she slipped the papers into her pocket. "But I didn't catch him. Nor am I the one who stopped him."

He shrugged. "But you found him."

Such logic would have made her laugh if she had the strength. "I think it was more along the lines of him finding me," she corrected him with a shake of her head. "It should be Mr. Thomas's money."

For a minute, Lucas just stared before shrugging and taking a step back. "He's had a hard past, and I don't know what you know, Miss Carlson. But I can assure you, money is far from his mind and he took no pleasure in killing another man. He wanted to keep you safe, and the knowledge that he saved you is more than enough for him, I'm sure. Consider it, and I'll return tomorrow for your answer." The sheriff turned to leave but paused first. "Get some rest, Miss Carlson, you've been through a lot."

His words made her think. Selina stared at the ceiling for hours, unable to fall sleep. All she could hear was the beating of her heart. It made her furious Wyatt had been there, and he'd saved her. She didn't want to depend on anyone for anything.

And she wondered why he'd come for her after their conversation. She'd been quite clear she wanted nothing else to do with him. Yet he had saved her from her uncle with little concern for his own safety. Now she owed him a great debt of gratitude and more.

So many mixed emotions and thoughts filled her mind until she couldn't take being alone anymore. There was too much in her head and she needed to talk to someone about everything. But there wasn't anyone. Selina decided she might try walking again. Her body screamed as she worked on sitting up at the edge of the bed. The bruising on her hip had grown swollen and numbed a good part of her leg.

"Come on, come on," she murmured, frowning as she managed to grab hold of the nearby chair. Using it as a crutch, Selina pulled herself up. A bead of sweat dripped by the time she made it, her arms trembling. Still leaning on the chair, she staggered to the wall, keeping her weight on her good leg.

Her breath caught as she opened the door and found no one there. Glancing at the floor, she knew it would take three steps at least to get across the hall and it suddenly felt as wide as a valley. Taking a deep breath, she stretched forward with one hand but couldn't reach it.

She'd have to make it without support. After gathering her strength, she made the lunge and banged a shoulder into the door, wincing.

"What is it?" A groggy voice came from the other side of the door and she froze.

Suddenly she wasn't certain she wanted to do this. How was she to face him? Glancing back at her room, Selina hesitated. The man had been seriously injured, almost died to protect her. He'd probably saved her life. She wondered if he'd want to see her after the things she'd said to him. Yet she still needed to talk to him, to be honest and only then would she know what to do. If nothing else, she owed him a word of thanks. After another deep breath, she slowly opened the door.

He was watching the door, waiting. One hand gripping the edge of the cot, ready to get up, and the other one hidden under the covers. Squinting, his eyes widened in surprise at the sight of her, and then he sighed as his entire body relaxed. "Selina," he breathed softly. "You're all right."

His words made her want to laugh, but she was too busy concentrating on the best strategy to get over to him. He had a larger room and there was a chair far off in the other corner. Taking a deep breath, she staggered, a hand on her hip, in his direction.

"We need to talk, I suppose." She started to get further into the room and she lost her balance when she put too much pressure on her bad leg.

But Wyatt was fast, and had an arm around her before she could fall, helping her to the edge of his bed. His gaze was too intense for her to meet, so she stared at the floor as she tried to catch her breath and wipe the sweat from her brow. "Selina? Are you all right?"

"Well, I think so." Her voice fell as she realized he wasn't wearing a shirt. Instantly she felt her face flush and she couldn't stop staring. Not so much at his muscular chest, though she did notice it. She saw the bandage on his shoulder, but it was the scars that held her attention. She recognized a few, from the stories he told her. In the middle of his ribs, were what looked to be burns that had faded from time. Selina almost reached out to touch them but she caught herself.

He took her hand and squeezed it, breaking her away from her thoughts. Taking a deep breath, Selina turned and slipped her hand away. She needed to focus, and she couldn't while he touched her with his kindness. Though she'd worried about the tension and awkwardness, she felt only easiness between them.

Carefully taking the papers from her pocket, she showed the poster of James to him. "There's a reward." She paused to clear her raspy voice. "For him."

Carefully, Wyatt unfolded the page and stared at it blankly. Chancing a look, Selina saw Wyatt had a black eye and a cut on his lip as well. His knuckles were bandaged, but the big concern was the bullet wound. Dr. Fitzgerald had told her it had torn through Wyatt's body, making a clean exit. But they had to keep an eye on infection, so he wouldn't be leaving for a while.

"It's yours," he said finally, and returned the paper to her. "I don't want it. I don't need it."

She frowned. "But you deserve it. You stopped him, you're the one."

Shaking his head, he raised a hand. "I said I don't want it, Miss Carlson. It would just be a reminder of him, no matter who he was or what he did. What he was trying to do will never leave my mind."

Her cheeks burned, and she looked away, feeling the sting of tears. Tears of humiliation, of pain, of guilt. Gulping, she sniffed and realized she wanted to tell him the truth. And now, what would it hurt since it was all over between them? He deserved that much, she supposed, and wiped her eyes.

"James," she started, and sucked in more air as she felt light-headed. When it passed, she began again. "James Robinson was my uncle. He married my mother's sister. After my parents died in the shootout, I lived with my grandmother until I lost her, too. I had no other family, so they sent met to live there with them. It wasn't a good place, but it was better than the streets. At least that's what I thought. I tried to escape him. I fought, and I fought, but he was stronger and bigger."

He put a hand on her shoulder comfortingly, but she still jumped. "You don't need to explain any of that."

She cut him off with a furious shake of the head. She had to get it out, and she'd already begun.

"Mary left me money and a note telling me to come here. She was afraid he'd kill me. So I did what she told me and I came here. I thought I'd be safe. I was so sure things would be good, and I could start over. I had no idea he would find me." The tears came and so she stopped, trying to catch her breath. Gulping, she shook her head at the paper. "I don't want it, Wyatt, please."

Chapter Twenty

He dropped the piece of paper so neither of them had to touch it. It was an ugly reminder neither wanted. Sniffling, Selina turned away and Wyatt glanced at his bandaged hands. "What shall we do with it?" he asked after a moment of silence. And after another stretch of silence he changed the subject. "What of your aunt?"

With a frown, she pulled out an unopened telegram and read it out loud. "*Sorry for everything Please forgive me Police know all Mary.*" She stared at it for a minute as the words sunk in. "He beat her again." Her voice was a whisper. "He injured her over and over. For years. I never thought of it much because neither of them treated me well. Since he beat me and she didn't stop him, it sort of felt like she deserved it. But I should have tried to help." She closed her eyes. "Yes, she should have it. When Mr. Jessup returns, I'll tell him to send it to Mary."

They fell quiet, and he leaned back against the wall, closing his eyes. He'd been shot before and the pain had already turned dull. And knowing with a surety Selina was safe helped relax the knots in his stomach. Wyatt had only awakened that morning after being out for a few days, and could feel the room spinning. With a soft groan, he allowed the exhaustion to take over.

Wyatt wasn't certain if it was the squeeze of the hand or the soft voice that woke him, but he felt it pulling him from the darkness. "You fool," a quiet voice murmured. "What were you thinking, attacking James? You could have died, Wyatt."

He took a deep breath and let it out slowly.

"You must be in such pain," Selina murmured, sniffling. "And then trying to rescue me after everything I said to you." Wyatt tried to open his eyes and wanted to ask her if she was talking to him, but his body felt sluggish. She didn't seem to notice. "You let me talk to you so horribly and then still came after me? What a gentleman, what a fool of a gentleman." She grew quiet and waited. She had his hand in hers, rubbing it lightly with a soft squeeze. "Perhaps I'm the fool. Letting you go, letting you think I don't care."

She raised his hand and kissed it gently. His eyes were still closed, and she took the chance to finish her thoughts.

"I do care, you know. I don't want to, but I do. I was so mad at you. But I was just so afraid you would leave for some reason. I thought it meant you weren't who I thought you were, and that frightened me. I liked the Wyatt I knew, and if he didn't really exist, then it meant I was alone. I didn't know what to do about that. I'm so sorry, Wyatt, I'm sorry."

He found the strength and squeezed her hand in return. It caught her by surprise and Selina yelped. Trying not to smile, Wyatt slowly opened his eyes at the confounded girl. She wrapped a hand around her heart, chest heaving in fright. "It's all right," he managed with a foolish grin.

"You were listening the whole time?" Her mouth dropped open and her cheeks turned bright red.

Groaning, Wyatt shook his head and tried to sit up. That's when the room started to spin and he stopped and with a grimace, he grudgingly collapsed back on the cot. Swallowing his pride, he took a deep breath and glanced at his bandaged shoulder. "Only some of it. But you were right. The other day, at my house, I should have been honest. Miss Carlson…"

She shook her head. "Selina."

He managed to smile. It hurt his cheek terribly, but to say her name again was a pleasure he couldn't resist. "Selina, I wasn't worried about telling you about my agreement with Mrs. Jessup because I didn't think it was a secret, and it wasn't something I wanted to hide." He tried to find the right words. "But I did want to hide something. I haven't been entirely honest because people don't always take it well when I tell them about my past. When I was sixteen, I joined up with Luis the Sixer. The bounty hunter. I worked as a hunter myself until I came here to start over. It was a hard, cruel life, and I did many things I'm not proud of. My actions often weren't honorable, and I wasn't a gentleman."

After everything, he expected her to leave the room, but nothing could have prepared Wyatt for Selina to bite her lip and then shake her head. "No matter what you think, you are a gentleman. In every sense of the word."

Wyatt could hardly believe it. Taking her hand, he kissed it gently as he marveled at her strength. "I'm trying to be. And if you'll have me, I'd like to be the gentleman you marry. As soon as I can stand up without getting dizzy." He smiled crookedly. "I love you, Selina, and I think you love me, too. Please tell me I'm not confused."

He had told her what was in his heart and he felt like he was walking into a gunfight with a white flag. This was new territory to him. He hadn't planned the words, but he knew he wouldn't regret telling her how he felt and what he wanted.

Now, he could only hope she felt the same. Wyatt watched Selina as she bit her lip. Rubbing her eyes, her cheeks grew splotchy, and she tried to laugh. It was a quiet laugh, a cute one, the one she gave any time she tripped or did something she thought was silly. Catching him by surprise, she covered his hand and raised it to her soft cheek.

Finally she smiled and nodded. "Yes," she whispered. "Yes, I'll marry you, Wyatt."

He let out a breath. "You had me worried for a minute." In spite of the pain it took to move, he pulled her close for a proper kiss. She leaned in to him without hesitation and his heart sang. His cut lip burned, but he didn't mind. Nothing but Selina and their happiness mattered now. He grinned so wide his entire face hurt. "We should get married tomorrow."

She pulled back as she gave him a look. "Tomorrow? Wyatt, you can't even walk. And I have this painful limp." She frowned as she tilted her head.

He thought back to how difficult it had been for her to just cross the room and knew she had a point. "Fine. Next week, then." He gave her a grin as she rolled her eyes.

Chapter Twenty-One

Selina and Wyatt's wedding happened four months and five days after he asked her to marry him. It took them both a week before they were well enough to make the journey home. Selina still walked with a slight limp but she'd made a wonderful recovery. Wyatt took some time to fully run his ranch again. He hired extra help during the harvest until he could use his arm again. But they were both well, and both safe.

"We're here!" Susannah hurried down the aisle, her husband trailing behind her. Straightening up, Wyatt shifted his stance and nodded as the couple sat down. If they were here, then it meant Selina was here.

"She's coming soon, Wyatt." Susannah beamed at him, her happiness seemed to bubble over. "It was just lovely weather you know, on the drive over. Just perfect, just perfect. Lucas, do you know what this reminds me of?"

Wyatt grinned at the bubbly woman. Her excitement was always infectious, and very appropriate. Chuckling, Lucas wrapped an arm around his wife. "Our own wedding, of course. But today isn't about us, Susie darling.

Let's focus first on getting these two kids happily married, shall we?"

"We shall!" Susannah nodded hurriedly and settled down as the back doors opened again.

She was very happy, Wyatt could tell. Selina had told him about her reconciliation with Susannah. After several long conversations, they'd repaired their relationship. Susannah was a wonderful woman who clearly tried her best. And all in all, there was a wedding that needed to be planned.

Selina entered the room, carefully shaking off her cloak and fixing her hold on her bouquet of white flowers and ivy. Selina was stunning, and he grinned as she finally met his gaze.

Eagerness had been driving him all day, and it all faded away as she hastened to join him by the pastor. Wyatt's hand went out to her, and she clutched it, not letting go. She ran a finger over his knuckles, now healed as though nothing had happened.

"Welcome, friends of Selina Carlson and Wyatt Thomas." The pastor started the ceremony, but Wyatt hardly paid attention. He was dressed in his best suit, and she had a new light blue dress for the occasion. The last four months had been some of the longest days of his life, but they had been some of the happiest.

They were both able to make complete recoveries though his shoulder was often sore, and she walked with just a bit of a limp. It would take time, Dr. Fitzgerald had assured them, but they were both strong people who would eventually heal completely.

The emotional healing had come, too. Together, they'd agreed to put their pasts behind them and start fresh together. This wasn't easy, and they'd spend hour after hour talking it through, but the progress was un-deniable.

She squeezed his hand, bringing him back to the present. Wyatt met her gaze with a grin.

"Do you, Selina Carlson, take Wyatt Thomas to be your lawfully wedded husband?"

"I do."

"Do you, Wyatt Thomas, take Selina Carlson to be your lawfully wedded wife?"

He squeezed her hand as she smiled up at him. "I do," he assured her, and pulled back the veil so he could finally kiss his wife.

As they shared their first kiss as husband and wife, Wyatt felt Selina relax. The joy at seeing her at peace and happy was a surprise. He'd never cared for another person this much before. He loved the feeling and he looked forward to making her happy and keeping her safe for the rest of his life.

"Let's get started on our life together, Selina. I'm so thankful God worked it out for us."

She smiled and looped her arm with his and walked with her husband out of the church as they approached their next adventure together.

* * * * *

CHRISTINA AND MITCHELL

Chapter One

Susannah

Christmas afternoon was as pretty as a painting. There was fluffy white snow in the mountains, across the fields, and on the window sills. Susannah Jessup leaned on the window frame and took another deep breath. It was simply refreshing. There was so much good to celebrate, and her heart was overflowing. Glancing up at the sky, she wondered if more snow would fall. Biting her lip, she tried to imagine anything more perfect.

"Silent night, holy night. This smells good, and all is light." She smiled as Lucas wrapped his arms around her from behind. "Merry Christmas, Susie darling. I didn't miss anything, did I?"

She rolled her eyes as he turned her around and kissed her forehead. This Christmas they'd prepared and planned to take goods to struggling families in Rocky Ridge. Though Susannah was supposed to go with him, she was recovering from a sprained ankle. Lucas had won the argument about her staying home to rest and prepare for their lunch party. Susannah let go of her disappointment as he bent down and picked her up.

Squealing in surprise, she grabbed his shirt and then laughed at his proud expression. His faded scar stretched beside his charming dimples and Susannah couldn't help with a kiss as she wound her arms around his neck. "Did everything work out all right?" she asked him as he carried her across the room.

He sat her down and checked on her ankle. The swelling was down, but he treated it as carefully in his lap as he treated the baby chicks they'd had just the other month. "Of course, dear. The deliveries went perfectly and I rode straight home."

Listening, she made a face when he poked her foot. "Ow! You can stop that, Lucas. And good. Thank you for doing that." She grabbed his hand with a grin. "I only wish I could have seen their faces. Everyone deserves a happy Christmas."

Chuckling, he leaned forward and gave her a kiss that made her blush. After all these years, he still knew how to make her heart skip a beat. Susannah curled up closer and sighed. He wrapped an arm around her as she suddenly yawned. "If you're too tired," he offered, "we don't need to have a party."

"What? No!" She straightened up. "No, I'm fine." He raised an eyebrow at her and so Susannah clambered up to her feet. "See?" And then she tried not to wince.

He only rolled his eyes. "You're too stubborn."

Susannah was about to say something when there was a knock at the door. "They're here! Lucas! Come, come!" She hobbled down the hall. He followed right behind her, and his long arm reached the doorknob first as the other wound around her hip. "Eleanor! Susie! Matthew! Come in, come in."

"It's good to see you, too," Eleanor chuckled in the tight hug Susannah gave her. "But if you don't mind, it's chilly outside." The ladies laughed as everyone piled into the house. After the hugs, Lucas wrapped a firm grip around Susannah's waist again to work as a crutch. They shared a quiet look and she nudged him sweetly.

The Connors had just settled down when there was another knock where they found the Jensens there. Jeb was helping Rowena off with her jacket. "Merry Christmas!" she cried out and accepted a big hug from Susannah. Rowena's large round belly was in the way, but no one minded.

"It's been too long. But I'm certainly glad you could make it," Susannah chuckled, ushering the couple in. "Jeb, I certainly hope you've been taking excellent care of these two?"

Jeb chuckled sheepishly, pulling off his hat as he hung up his wife's cloak. "I wouldn't dream of disappointing you. Or her," he added with a wink to Rowena. "Which is why she should probably sit down now," Jeb continued, and helped his wife to a comfortable seat.

The scent of cider and cinnamon wafted through the house as Susannah served her guests the delicious warm drinks. Eleanor and Matthew were retelling a silly story from their first Christmas as there was another knock at the door. Lucas stood to go, but Susannah set the platter down with a shake of her head. She was too excited to let the hobbling slow her down. The door opened to reveal the Jameses and the Thomases.

"Merry Christmas!" they all cried out together as if they'd planned the greeting.

Simon was holding the new baby, Joseph, and Susannah took him in her arms the moment she was done providing hugs. Olivia beamed at her husband and wandered inside as Wyatt stood over his wife protectively and helped her off with her jacket. "It's good to see you, Susannah," Selina murmured breathlessly. "My, it's chilly today."

"Chilly? It's freezing," Wyatt corrected her with a chuckle. "You're wearing all three of your coats." Only once they were taken off did the two women hug with baby Joseph between them.

Susannah stepped back and sized up the couple. They had only been wed a few weeks and their newlywed closeness was touching. "Oh, you two are just swell," she murmured with a happy sigh. "Come in. We're all here and I'll bring out the food."

Selina hurried after her once the babe was handed over to Lucas. "Let me help," she offered. "I still know my way around the kitchen. What can I do to help?" And she was already grabbing an apron.

Twirling around in surprise, Susannah shook her head. "No, you don't need to. Please, Selina, it's time you enjoyed yourself. You should be out there with our friends. And the children," she added brightly.

But the woman shrugged. "That's all right." Selina managed a tight smile. "Here, let me grab that. Besides, Wyatt and I… I mean, we do want a family. He wants children, I'm sure. But… I mean, I can wait, so that's all right. I can help you."

The words caught Susannah's attention, or more the way the other woman was saying them. Frowning, she clutched the bowl of potatoes and studied her. "What's going on?" She frowned. She set the food on the table and fixed two of the glasses before turning to Selina. "Is something the matter? You don't sound as excited as, well, I thought a young woman would sound speaking about her future."

Setting down napkins, the young woman pulled her braid back and sighed. "I will be, I'm sure. With time. Is it normal? Are all married women thrilled at the prospect of children? That is, I would love to have one, especially with Wyatt. I only…well, I've never spent time with children." As she talked, Selina began to pace, and Susannah realized it was a serious concern.

Yet it didn't need to be. "Stop." Susannah grabbed the woman by the arms carefully. Though the younger woman was much taller, her shy gaze made her appear small. Helping her into a seat, the blonde sighed. "A family is a beautiful and wonderful thing, whether it's just the two of you or more. Even if you haven't had much experience with children, that will come. And you have friends in the other room more than willing to teach you. A family should be taken seriously, but goodness Selina, you're too young to worry about this."

The young woman avoided her gaze. "Wyatt said the same thing. I just thought he was…well, Wyatt tends to be a little more hopeful than I am."

Trying to imagine that, Susannah laughed. Wyatt was a serious man, used to a hard and dangerous life. In fact, they both were. But Rocky Ridge had become their home and they had found each other. "You two are silly, but you have a bright future ahead of you. And I doubt that children always come into our lives at the perfect moment. Keep that in mind."

The girl hesitated and squeezed Susannah's hand. "Can I ask you something? You and Lucas have never had any children, but you do so well with them. How do you know how to hold a baby and swaddle them? And the feeding. Oh my, how do you learn these things?"

It was the holidays and her heart was full. Susannah couldn't resist wrapping the young woman in a tight hug. Selina hesitantly returned it. "You don't," Susannah told her finally. "You can't know anything until you try." She pulled away and grabbed the woman's hands. "And for what it's worth, I think you'd be a wonderful mother. Selina, you're a sweet woman who is sensitive and strong. You just need to have faith in yourself. Now, go out there and meet Joseph. He has the softest hair, it'll make you want to cry." Susannah beamed and ushered the woman back out there.

She was nearly finished setting the table when Lucas strolled in. He walked with purpose, but paused to watch her walk. Susannah could feel his gaze on her as she went limping back and forth. Usually he said something right away, but he didn't do a thing. Finally, she stopped and crossed her arms. "You're distracting me, Lucas," she told him. "Are you going to help me or remain a hindrance?"

Running a hand through his dark hair, he finally blinked and refocused his gaze. "It's a good Christmas, isn't it?"

Susannah walked over and touched his cheek. "It's a very good Christmas, Lucas. One of the best." Standing on the tips of her toes, she kissed his cheek where her right hand had just been, hoping that might help. "You're worried about the babies, aren't you?"

His hesitation was enough and she sighed. It had made her nervous earlier that morning as well. Her husband looked wearier than usual and her heart went out to him as she squeezed his hands comfortingly. "Dear… It's Christmas, and we're surrounded by our friends. I'm happy and I know you're happy, too. What we have, Lucas, is enough. I promise." She kissed his hands. They were rough and scarred from his years as a Ranger, and she loved every part of him.

Slowly he wrapped his arms around her and kissed her forehead. Her matchmaking venture was well underway and she was happy with her success so far. Though there had been hardships and complications, things had come together. And now, they were with good friends ready to celebrate the year and she was already looking forward to what the next year would bring.

"Good," he murmured. "Let's get this party started, then, shall we?"

Chapter Two

Christina

It was a busy afternoon, and there probably wouldn't be enough potatoes. Christina Bristol blew a strand of hair from her face and tied off a full sack before shifting it to her left. There, it sat on the wagon's edge and waited for her Uncle Steven to come pick it up.

"How are you doing over here?" He arrived with a grin. "And I need three more."

"Three?" She shook her head in disbelief and moved hurriedly to shift the boxes around to grab more. "Uncle! We're down to five boxes. I knew we should have brought the last ten. Didn't I say that? We could have sold them and I know they're still green, but it would have been a profit. Why didn't I put them on the wagon?"

Chuckling, the man stroked his beard and winked as he took the bags. "Because, dear, they wouldn't fit in the wagon. You know, we're finishing up but we could still use some help in the front of our stall. Why don't you join your mother and start counting the change?"

The smile froze on her face as she was in the middle

of shifting the boxes around. She could feel her jaw lock and Christina glanced around. It was a sunny day in the middle of winter at the town market. At this time of the year there wasn't much for sale out here. But thanks to a few savvy tricks and a lot of hard work and commitment, they managed to have potatoes year-round.

And though it was cold, there were still plenty of townsfolk out and about. People were talking and laughing and wandering everywhere. She recognized several faces. Now the idea of going out there made her stomach ache.

"I don't know," she began hesitantly. "These sacks need to be filled, and I'm not that good at counting. I'm sure Mother is doing fine without me." She looked down at her hands. They were ungloved to better handle the potatoes and knew folks wouldn't take kindly to them. They may not take kindly to her, either.

His gaze drifted down to her hands, too. He took both her hands and squeezed them with a grin so big it stretched from ear to ear. "Nonsense. A little fresh air will do you good. Don't you worry about anyone. They don't know what they're saying most of the time anyway. Fill that sack and come help me take these to the Jeffersons, won't you?"

The man was as friendly as he was stubborn. Christina obeyed and found herself climbing out of the wagon and into the sunlight. Snow crunched beneath her boots as she glanced around, squinting in the brightness. It was a lovely day, she acknowledged, and it would have been silly to let it pass her by untouched.

"All right." She took a deep breath and gathered her courage. "Where is the Jefferson wagon?" She hefted her sack up in her arms, taking a deep breath as she looked around the area. After five steps out in the open, she could already feel the itch across her skin and the tingle on her spine.

Ignore it, she told herself. It doesn't matter. Biting her tongue, Christina kept her gaze down and stared at the steps her uncle took as he stomped along. She copied, following in his steps to keep down the effort of creating a new path in the snow. Even then it was a struggle, and Christina tried her best to keep up with him.

"Here you are," Uncle Steven proclaimed loudly. "This should last you for a while. All those kids of yours will be fed quite nicely, I think. If you need any new ideas of how to use these potatoes, my Ruby has a few good recipes she'd be happy to share with you. She's quite inventive with potatoes, that woman!"

Mrs. Jefferson had been moving things around in their small cart, one with two wheels instead of four and it held very little. Her husband was ready to pay, and she turned to them with a big smile that faded when she noticed the younger woman.

Christina's stomach dropped as well and immediately she ducked her head, turning it ever so slightly hoping her hair would fall down as a drape to hide her face. Holding up the sack higher than before, she used it as a barrier and peace offering. Mrs. Jefferson's face tightened like she'd smelled something foul as she snatched the bag away from her. "Wonderful." She scowled. "These'll need an extra wash. Just in the cart, Mr. Ennis. That will be all."

Christina shoved her hands into her coat pockets and turned away, moving as fast as she could without running. As Uncle Steven said farewell she returned to their stall. Heat climbed up her neck and spread across her cheeks as she kept her head low, and found herself bumping into her mother.

The tall willowy blonde grabbed her arm. "There you are, Christina. We could use your help. Do you mind picking up five pounds of pork at the butcher's?" Jane Bristol was a beauty even though she was in her late thirties. Men still watched her in the street, and she could charm her way through nearly anything. There was little, clearly, that Christina had in common with her mother.

The woman had told her she took after her father, in looks and gentle manners. It would have been nice, perhaps, if he had been around to prove this. But at the looks Christina received as she clutched the money in her hands and walked down the street, she wasn't certain having him here would be good. The two of them would never have been welcome in this town even with Jane to protect them.

Unable to deny her mother anything, Christina ducked her head again and grudgingly headed down the street. The afternoon was windy and blew her coal-black hair all about. She considered tying it into a comfortable braid, but they would still judge her whether it blew around her face or was shaved off.

"Just look at her," she heard children murmuring by the schoolhouse. "The strange one. She's not one of us."

"Where did she come from? I heard she was raised by bears."

Christina started to walk faster, further down the street. But the wind was strong and it still carried the voices her way. "You can't trust people like her. They aren't really people. They're savages."

"Mother says she isn't allowed to play with fire, in case she burns their house down. And Father said she talks to horses. Just like the Apache. The Apache are devils, and so is she."

That one caught her breath. Her stomach churned, and she felt the bile trying to rise in her throat, but she swallowed it down and kept walking. Almost there, Christina told herself, she was almost there.

It was only down the road but it felt like it took forever. She hadn't realized how shallow her breath was until she stepped inside and inhaled deeply. Her head felt light as she blinked in the dimness and glanced around.

The shop was small and there were only two other people there besides herself and the owner, Maryn. He was talking to the other two men and shot her a curt glance as she entered. She tried to wave for attention, but he turned away. Her relief was short-lived. "Ex-excuse me?" she asked politely. "Hello?" She cleared her throat and tried to speak louder each time. "Excuse me? Might I make a purchase? Please?"

Once her voice was louder, Maryn didn't have a choice. But he wasn't happy about having to acknowledge her. "I'm trying to have a conversation. Can't you see that?"

She took an involuntary step backwards. With a shaky breath, she knew she wouldn't have any support from the other two men staring at her. It made her uncomfortable and her palms began to sweat. The heat rose to her cheeks, but she didn't know what to do about it. She never did, no matter how often this happened.

"I'm sorry, but I'm in need of some pork. It's for my uncle." She hesitated, worried they wouldn't give her the right amount again. The butcher had shorted her and taken her money last time. "Five pounds, please."

Maryn scoffed but he took the sale, snatching the money as he handed over the meat. He gave no inclination that he was going to give her the change due and she didn't know what to do. So, she just left. With the pork wrapped up under her arm, Christina hurried back into the cold. This time the streets were empty and so her walk back to the market and her family was pleasant.

"There you are," Jane began but started to cough. It was a thick one, and Christina's smile slipped as she patted her mother's back in concern. She hadn't heard anything so terrible in a while, and she glanced around for some water when it suddenly stopped. Her mother chuckled, patting her chest. "I'm sorry about that. I think I've had too much fresh air today. Now, did you get the meat?"

Nodding, Christina gave her mother a tight smile. "Yes, I did. There wasn't any change, I'm afraid."

"No? Strange. Perhaps things are tight for Maryn," Jane mused, and turned to her sister. Ruby was shorter than Christina and shrugged. "How strange, and I thought his business was booming. Winter is always a difficult season, however. Thank you, Christina. I think we're done for the day, Ruby. Shall we pack up?"

Soon they were on their way home. Christina sat on an empty box in the back, watching the town grow smaller in the distance as she rested against her mother's shoulder. Her mother nudged her. "You're quieter than usual. What's wrong, Christina?"

She bit her lip, unable to meet her mother's gaze. "Oh, it's nothing, Mother. I was just thinking, well, wondering actually. Was Father an Apache? I know you don't like talking about him." Christina straightened and moved on quickly. "I was just wondering because I heard them saying things. You said he was a good man and I'm not sure what to believe."

Jane squeezed her arm firmly. The concerned expression made the girl bite her tongue and she swallowed hard. "What did they say? Christina, oh, I wish you wouldn't listen to them. But it's not your fault. It's not yours, nor your father's fault. People can be so cruel, they don't know what they're saying." She brushed the hair from Christina's face. "No, your father wasn't an Apache. He was Sioux, as a matter of fact. And a gentleman, no matter what they say."

Christina looked at her mother and blinked, trying to understand it all.

"I don't talk about him because it hurts. Oh, but I do wish you could have met him. He'd have loved you so much." Christina's mother inhaled deeply. "Folks might think they're good people but wearing the newest bonnets means nothing if they aren't charitable on the inside. A person's outward appearance doesn't matter as much as what's in their hearts."

The wagon came to a stop and they were home. Jane grabbed her daughter's hand before they moved. "Christina, I'm very proud of the young woman you've become. You're a wonderful, wise, and beautiful girl."

"If I'm so beautiful, why don't they accept me?"

"The right people will accept you," her mother assured her. "Trust in God, and you'll find the love you deserve. Besides me, of course." She chuckled, and kissed her daughter's head. "Now let's go inside."

She coughed deeply as they clambered out of the wagon and cleaned up the boxes before heading inside. At first Christina thought nothing of that, but by the end of the week her mother could hardly stand up without a coughing fit.

Chapter Three

Mitchell

"Whoa, there!" Mitchell Powell pulled on his horse's reins to bring them to a stop. Standing straight up in the saddle, the tall man looked about warily. He thought he'd seen some movement but couldn't be certain. Glancing at the horse, he watched his head turn and his ears flick. Until they stopped, and the horse pawed the ground impatiently, ready to move again. "Are you certain?" he asked his horse with a chuckle. "Well, if you say so. Hiyah!"

The Appaloosa was young and loved the wide-open country. It was the middle of winter but the sun had been out and melted much of the snow in the last two days. He loosened the reins and leaned in, letting the animal take the lead as they headed down the trail. It was good for the horse to stretch his legs and get a feel for the ground below them.

With the sharp chill in the air, his eyes watered as they sped over the land. But he didn't mind, used to the cold. Granted, he allowed, it was still colder than he thought it would be. And they said the worst of winter was already over. Yet if the town of Rocky Ridge could survive a Colorado winter every year, so could he.

It was a nice town, even nicer than Colorado Springs and Boston combined. Mitchell and his horse followed the path through the avenue and they rounded the last of herd in the east before making it back to Harrison. The old man was slumped in his saddle, smoking and humming some old song as he glanced about warily.

"Any sign of them Injuns?" Harrison grumbled.

Mitchell shook his head. "Of course not. They aren't what we need to worry about. We just need to make sure our horns stay with the herd this time around."

With a heavy sigh, the man tugged on his scarf and pulled it up over his mouth. His thick mustache was tinged with white frost. Shaking his head, the old man grumbled something under his breath. Mitchell raised his eyebrow at the man who made a face and turned his horse to the side. His muffled voice was louder this time. "You can take a break. Go to town, do what you want. Just get out of here. I got the herd for the evening."

"Watch by yourself?" Mitchell shook his head. "I don't think that's wise. Besides, there's no reason for me to go into town. I don't know what I would do there anyway."

But the man was obstinate. "The twins are headed back any minute and will help me keep watch for the night. You've been working mornings, nights, everything. At least take the rest of the day off. Then you can sleep with the cows for all I care. But right now, you're not working."

For a minute, Mitchell considered arguing. Why, if he needed to, he could take the old man. He was tough and good with a gun, but the other man hadn't wres-

tled or been in a fight in years. Just as his fists were
clenching, the younger man realized he was being ridiculous. Harrison was trying to be generous by giving
him some time away from the trail. "Fine," he muttered,
and turned his horse away.

Their enthusiasm dampened as they headed into
town, the man and his ride. He wandered through
the streets, keeping his head low and his collar high.
Rocky Ridge was small, but it was spread out and full
of vibrant colors. If there was any nice place on Earth,
Mitchell decided, this could be it. But all the same, he
didn't think testing the limits would be the best move.

A mercantile caught his eye, and that reminded him
he needed some buttons. Grudgingly he brought the
horse to a stop and climbed down. Mitchell carefully
eyed his surroundings, making sure he and his horse
wouldn't have a reason for leaving in a hurry. "Stay
put," he ordered, and was just grabbing his hat to put it
back on his head when he caught sight of two children
with their mother passing him on the street.

It would have been an ordinary sight had the boy not
suddenly dropped his mouth wide open with a stare.
Mitchell met his gaze, and he felt the slight glimmer of
excitement of being in town fade away. Even after all
this time, no matter where he went, some things just
never changed. Staring wasn't necessarily mean and
not even a crime, but it had a way of tying his stomach
in knots and making him feel ashamed.

Turning up his collar again, he pulled the hat back
down and looked away. That way, Mitchell's face would
be completely hidden from the boy's view. A moment
later, he could hear the mother talking to her children,

telling them to move along. Soon they were gone, and it was as though it had never happened. Almost.

Mitchell thought seriously about turning around. He didn't really need to be here. But he was right there at the shop, and he knew he needed to get it over with. In and out, he told himself, and all would be fine. Then he'd be back on the job where he belonged. His team knew him and accepted him as he was.

Still, he kept the hat on when he stepped inside. For a moment, he stood quietly and took in the cinnamon scent and enjoyed being somewhere else besides a campfire site with his countrymen. Sometimes he forgot how nice it could be when people settled down. Moving around in the store, Mitchell leaned down and traced a glove over a few ribbons. Perhaps he could get a few for his mother?

He stopped. It had happened again. He dropped his hand and moved away. It was the one thing he had enjoyed about going into towns during the cattle drives over the years. The ability to always find something new to send to his mother back in Boston was a treat. He'd left home when he was sixteen and liked to find little gifts to mail so she knew he hadn't forgotten her.

But just about a year ago, she'd grown sick and he'd lost her. His mother didn't need ribbons in Heaven.

"They're pretty nice, eh? Better than what you can find in Colorado Springs, any day." A voice sounded beside him, and Mitchell froze. Another man, a few years older than himself, looked at him with a grin as he picked up a spool. "Do you think this is pink enough?"

Mitchell didn't understand him for a minute. "I, um, I suppose." Shifting his weight onto the other foot, he shrugged hesitantly. "But I wouldn't know."

The man laughed, making his hat only sit more crookedly than before on his head. "Neither would I. I always tell Eleanor if she really insists on me going out to make the purchases, she needs to be happy with what I bring home. That is, unless she isn't happy and that's when I come back and trade things out." He winked. "I'm Matthew, by the way. Matthew Connor. How are you?"

Shaking his hand, Mitchell waited for the inevitable moment of staring, but the man hardly seemed to notice. "Hello. I'm Mitchell. Mitch Powell."

"Good to meet you." Matthew tipped his hat with a grin and after a moment of glancing at the options, he traded the spool for a softer pink. "This should do," he proclaimed after inspecting it carefully. "That way, if little Susie tries putting her ribbons on my cattle again, then they'll still look mighty fine." And he laughed like it was a joke, slapping his knee.

"You work a herd here?" Mitchell glanced around curiously. "Where's your spread? I didn't think there was a lot out here."

Matthew shrugged. "Oh, there's plenty. This part of town, that's only half the folks. Now my place is a little closer towards Colorado Springs, so I don't come this way too often. But there's plenty of space in these hereabouts. You just passing through?"

They started to walk around, and Mitchell spotted the collection of buttons. "Yes." He nodded after a moment. "I'm driving a herd through. Job closes in Wyoming, and we should be heading out tomorrow, I believe."

"Have you worked them for a while?" Matthew asked curiously. "I haven't seen any other folks bringing their horns around here lately. At least not in this weather."

He smiled wryly. "It's a little mad, I know. Our foreman, Nichols, is as green as summer grass and thought we could move more slowly and make it work. I told him several times we'd need to beat the snow, but I'm afraid there's no moving some folks."

Matthew nodded knowingly. "I've been there. That's why you've got to eventually go to work for yourself. It's harder, but at least your problems are all your own. Have you any plans after Wyoming? Are you waiting on another herd, or what?"

That sort of question arose often enough, but Mitchell just shrugged. It was the west, after all. "I've got a few prospects. I'm not certain, but there's always a job somewhere."

"Five yards, please." Matthew grinned at the man at the register and eyed Mitchell curiously for a moment. There was something about the man, his ease of conversation and casual enthusiasm. Mitchell wasn't sure if he'd ever met a man who appeared so relaxed. "Then how about you come work for me?"

Chapter Four

Christina

They caught the pneumonia too late, and within two weeks Christina's Uncle Steven prepared a plot for Jane Bristol beneath their old apple tree. There was a small grave marker beside it, one for her father as well. It was only a small cross made of sticks, not even a name in case others saw it. No one would have let it stay up if they knew who was buried there.

Two weeks passed, and Christina found herself frequently returning to the two graves. Her aunt and uncle gave her time and solitude, only making sure she was inside after dark. If she wasn't inside cooking, then that's where she would be.

"Christina! Supper time!"

She offered a shrug to show she'd heard, but didn't turn towards the house. The sky was overcast and she could hardly make out her mother's name carved out on the tree. Kneeling beside it, she traced her fingers over the name. She was becoming numb with the realization that her mother was gone.

"Dear?" Her aunt came up behind her. "Aren't you hungry?"

Christina's throat constricted. Food was the last thing on her mind. "No, I'm sorry. I'm not hungry." Her mother wouldn't be at the table, telling her what a good cook she was. Her mother wouldn't be there to help clean up afterwards. Just the idea of eating made her feel ill.

"But…" Her aunt hesitated, and gingerly set a hand on her shoulder. It was a pale hand that only reminded Christina of her mother. "Sweetheart, you haven't eaten anything today. Please, it's going to rain so let's get you inside. For me?"

Several moments passed until Christina relented. She stood up without the offered hand and stepped right out of reach. The warm touch had become unfamiliar to her, and she crossed her arms so that her Aunt Ruby wouldn't try to interlink them with hers. The walk back to the house felt long and it began to rain before they made it.

"There's my two ladies," Steven chuckled, coming forward with cloths. "Let's get you nice and dry for supper, shall we?" He handed them over. She listened to them laugh as she slowly patted herself dry and forced herself to eat a few bites before retiring for the evening.

Just as she was curling up on the bed, there was a knock at her door. Christina curled up into a ball, holding her mother's pillow. "Yes?" She sighed only wanting to be alone.

"It's Uncle Steven," he called. "I wanted to see if you'd like to join us at church tomorrow? It should be a nice day. And you haven't been since…well, in a while," the man finished awkwardly.

Christina pushed her hair out of her face. Dark hair, dark skin, and dark eyes, all of which set her apart from just about every person in town. All her life they'd watched and judged her. The only comfort she'd had was returning to her mother's side who assured her that she was a good human being with a good heart, and that they weren't right. Her heart was what truly mattered.

How could she go into town with no one to protect her from the stares? The mere idea made her hiccup and she bit her lip, burrowing deeper beneath her blanket. Her aunt and uncle were good people, but they didn't know how to protect her.

"No," she called out. "I'll watch the farm. Good night." Then Christina laid there through the night, trying to get some rest. No matter how much time she spent in bed, it never seemed to be enough sleep. Every day she grew more exhausted, and by the time she awoke on Sunday, her aunt and uncle had already left for Sunday services.

Wrapping a shawl around her shoulders, she wandered around the house. It was a nice house, one that Steven's parents had built. Ruby had married him when Christina was ten years old, and he had brought in all three women. He was a good man, with a good home. Ruby was fortunate. And in turn, Christina knew that she was.

She just couldn't feel it anymore. She was too miserable to feel fortunate, even to feel sad anymore. A lump formed in her throat, and there was a small realization in the back of her mind that things were bad. Though her aunt and uncle were managing their pain, she was not. Sniffling, Christina turned back to her room.

Although the plan was to return under the blankets, she noticed her mother's Bible on the table and picked it up before falling onto the pillow. A small spark of inspiration hit, and Christina wondered if the words might provide her some comfort. She had just opened the book when a piece of paper fell out. Frowning, she picked it up.

It looked like part of a newspaper, a clipping that had been carefully placed in there. Christina was confused, having never noticed it before though her mother had been the one to read aloud when they were together.

It was an advertisement. *Boarding House in Rocky Ridge, Colorado, for brides coming west. Women only. Board, meals, and lessons provided. Cheap. See the Jessups.* Confused, she read it over several times until it finally began to sink in. An offer for mail-order brides.

She dropped the paper like it was hot and the Bible quickly slid from her grip. Had her mother wanted to send her off to be married? The Bible lay there on the floor, mocking her. Swallowing hard, Christina burrowed under the covers. Squeezing her eyes shut, she tried to tell herself that she was only imagining this.

But as the next week passed, Christina couldn't stop thinking about what she'd found. She worked hard to keep away from the Good Book, ignoring it and hopping over it. This gave her the energy she needed to stay out of the room and slowly return to her duties. While she couldn't find the strength to go outside past the graves, she returned to the kitchen and started cooking again. It gave her the time she needed to think.

"They called him a horse thief," her mother had told her one evening, a few days before she died. "They wanted to hang him, but we had a good sheriff then. Since no one could prove it, he said that he couldn't be touched. He told me his name was Running Water, or at least that was the one I could pronounce." She had chuckled at that, and it had turned into a coughing fit.

Christina had brought her a glass of water. "You shouldn't speak, Mother. You need to regain your strength."

Mother had shaken her head. "Nonsense. It's time I told you this story, Christina. I've kept it to myself for far too long. Do you know what he called me when we met?"

Christina bit her bottom lip and shook her head.

"Ehawee. That means Laughing Maiden. Oh, he was so handsome. You remind me of him so much, and I'm so grateful for that. It's comforting to see a little of him when I look at you."

Touching her dark hair, Christina smiled.

"We only had two years, and he was often away with his people until they discovered he was visiting me. When they sent him away, Running Water told me it was worth it for the life we would have together. He promised to build me a home, and we would go west after you were born. We were wed after his way, by a spiritual leader of his people who married us in secret. No pastor would have ever done it for us, but he was a good friend to your father and never told a soul. It was a lovely ceremony, surrounded by flowers and under an apple tree. You would have loved it, Christina."

She could hear the love in her mother's voice, even through the exhaustion taking over her body. Her mother smiled and stroked her cheek. Her fingers were chilly, and Christina pulled her hand between hers, rubbing it for warmth. "What was he like?"

"Charming, and he had such a way with horses. That's how we met, you know. I went out riding further than usual and was turned around. I was lost, and it grew late. My horse threw a shoe, and he found me.

His English wasn't very good, but he built me a fire and gave me his blanket. We spent all night exchanging words as best we could until the sun came up. After Running Water helped my horse back to his feet, he brought me home. I made him supper in gratitude, and then he began stopping by our home nearly every day.

"It terrified Ruby at first, but he was charming and sweet. When she realized how much I cared for him, then she accepted him and came to care for him very much. He loved you, do you know that?"

Tears stung in the corners of her eyes, and Christina had sniffed, hiding her face in her mother's blanket. It only made her sadder, to know how good things had been before she was born. "But I don't remember him."

Her mother patted her head tenderly. "When I told him that you were on your way, he shouted for joy. I laughed so hard that I cried. I was worried that he would be mad, or that something bad would happen. But oh, he was so happy. The day you were born, he told me that your cries were those of a warrior maiden. You were christened as our Christina, but you were Mahpiya to him."

Christina had not heard that before. Her heart hammered in her chest as she peered up at her mother, those red-rimmed eyes and shaky hands. "Mahpiya? What does that mean?"

The woman was growing drowsy and her breathing was ragged. "The clouds and the sky." Her mother had yawned. "And our Heaven. You were our Heaven, dear." She drifted to sleep then, and her body had caved to the fever. Christina sat there all night, pondering her mother's words.

Jane had only wanted the best for her. Standing at

the table, looking at the three plates that were set out for supper, Christina slowly realized that the advertisement wasn't a problem. Her mother wanted her to have happiness, the joy she'd experienced with Running Water. She wanted her to be cared for. And they all knew she wouldn't find anything good in Virginia.

"I'm leaving," Christina announced softly that evening. She took a deep breath as her aunt and uncle looked at each other. The young woman slid the newspaper clipping across the table. "To Colorado."

Ruby stared at it for a long moment before she handed it to Steven. "Are you certain?"

"Yes." Christina nodded. "I think it might be the best thing, for all of us. I won't be in your way, and…and I need a fresh start. I found it in Mother's Bible and I think she wanted this for me. Thank you so much for raising me, for helping us, for everything. But I think it's best that I go." Her voice cracked and she looked away.

Ruby hurried around the table, grabbing Christina in her arms with tears in her eyes. She had been a big sister to Christina, and she realized she had never been without her aunt. The woman reminded her again of her mother, and they wept quietly, clinging to each other. Though it went unsaid, they all knew Christina couldn't have stayed there forever.

"We'll buy your ticket," Steven sighed, a lingering sadness in his voice. "And no matter what, you're always welcome back here if anything changes or goes wrong. You know this, right, Christina? You're family. We love you so very much."

Chapter Five

Mitchell

Mitchell stopped and cocked his head, wondering if he'd heard right. While he had heard plenty of strange things in the past, he wasn't sure how to acknowledge this. Frowning, he rubbed his ear and looked at the man he barely knew. "Pardon me?"

But Matthew Connor wasn't fazed and shrugged as though it were nothing. Perhaps he was the type of man to hand out jobs whenever he felt like doing so. "You sound smart and you seem like a man who keeps to himself. I need a good hand and if you need a job, I can give you one. In fact, my last foreman just quit because he couldn't take the cold. I don't blame him," Matthew added sheepishly, "but it was mighty inconvenient."

Their items were paid for before Mitchell could find his voice. Trying to sort this out, he squinted at the man to see if this was a joke. "You'd just give me a job, no questions asked?"

Matthew chuckled. "How about this, Mitch? You come out and see my spread if you're not doing anything else today. See the layout, have some supper, and we can talk expenses. You're under no obligation or anything. What do you say?"

While he wasn't certain what he had said in response to that, Mitchell found himself climbing back onto his horse, newly bought buttons tucked away, and following Matthew Connor out of town. It was an hour's ride away but he didn't mind. The fresh air did him good, and the tension eased from his shoulders.

And the man kept to his word. After reaching the Circle C ranch, Mitchell met the man's wife, Eleanor, and two children before heading up the hill to see the layout of the land. It was a nice place, but there was much work to be done. Most of it was still wild and could be better partitioned off to prepare for possible droughts and planting. The ranch was swell, and Mitchell helped the other ranch hands corral the cows before stopping for supper.

"I'll double that," Matthew offered later that evening, after a delicious supper and the two of them were enjoying the fireplace with coffee in hand. "I'll double what you've been paid, and you've got board in back with the other men. Two meals a day and food for your horse. You're an impressive gentleman and I like the way you work. Have we got a deal?"

Mitchell grinned and shook hands before he found himself telling Harrison later that evening that he was quitting. Somehow, he'd found a place to stay for a longer period than just a few nights. It was a new concept for him, but everything about the Circle C ranch and Matthew Connor felt right. The old man had given him a good long look and took several deep breaths on his rolled-up cigarette before saying anything.

"About time," Harrison drawled, to his surprise. "Best of luck, boy. The other drivers are gonna be mighty unhappy," he added with a chuckle. "Oh boy, now they might have to start carrying their weight around here!"

He left the man still laughing to himself and went to tell the rest of the lot. The other cattle drivers grumbled at his departure in the morning, but they otherwise parted on good terms. After his last night with the group, he collected his final pay, and they all went their separate ways. The cattlemen headed towards Wyoming and Mitchell went towards the Circle C. And his new future.

"Just the two of us now, Rascal." He sighed as he looked around at the clear skies and stroked his horse's neck as they went. "It'll be a mighty big change, but I'm hoping things go well."

The horse jerked his head as though he were listening, and Mitchell chuckled. Together they drove down the road, enjoying the sun on their faces. Matthew gave them the afternoon to get settled, and Mitchell put his horse in the stable with the intent to explore.

"Howdy, I'm Kyle." A young man waved from a fence where several of the men were watching someone in the ring. Kyle had a lazy smile and long limbs, and the man in the ring was short and portly. Neither of them were a match for the stallion in the ring that was prancing anxiously to evade capture. Mitchell paused and went over, tipping his hat to Kyle and the other men.

"Howdy," he said finally. "New horse to break in?"

The young man nodded, and Mitchell decided he couldn't be older than eighteen. The rest of the men were at differing points in their lives, a few in their forties and a few near his age. Seven men hung outside the ring, hooting and hollering to the man in the center, a man named Ellis. They cheered him on and Mitchell studied the scene before him carefully.

"He's a little older," Kyle was saying, "but Matthew liked the look of the horse and purchased him with the other wild ones. You need good horses for a sprawl like this, after all, and there's several more where this one came from."

He nodded carefully but frowned when Ellis pulled out a whip. "Is Mr. Connor putting anyone in charge of the horses here? To train them, I mean?"

Kyle shrugged, not really understanding. "We all take turns."

"Like that?" Mitchell asked in disbelief as Ellis started playing with the whip. On his first attempt, it flung back and hit his backside. He jumped, and the other men roared with laughter. Shaking his head, Mitchell suppressed the urge to stay back in the shadows unnoticed because he couldn't allow an animal to suffer like that. Immediately he hopped over the fence.

"Hey now," Kyle called out in protest. "It's not your turn!"

But that didn't matter. The other men shouted out as well, but Mitchell blocked them out. Frowning, he set his hat back and waved an arm to Ellis. The man realized he was there and stared as he fumbled unfamiliarly with the whip. "What's going on?" he said in an injured tone. "I'm not done yet."

"Yes, you are," Mitchell told him. "Now hand that over." Gritting his teeth, he snatched the whip and tossed it outside the ring. "Now get out of here." Ellis was too stunned to do anything else, and staggered back, eyeing him suspiciously. The other men were still calling out, but he wasn't listening.

People could be like that. Obstinate, selfish, and they'd do anything for attention. Pulling his hat off, he hung it on a post and turned to the horse in the corral who was still jerking around and pawing the ground. He was anxious in this confined space, scared and uncontrollable. It wasn't helping to have strangers shouting at him, either. Mitchell knew how he felt and kept his hands low and splayed near his waist as a gesture of good will.

"Hey, fellow," he murmured. "Hey now, it's all right. It's going to be just fine." Keeping his voice level, Mitchell started walking around the horse, inching closer but at an angle that didn't make it look like he was actually heading towards him.

It took work, of course. But soon the men quieted down, watching his strategy. Mitchell talked softly in a soothing tone and managed to get nearly within arm's reach before the horse rallied, kicked up his legs, and trotted in the other direction. But he would be prevented from jumping the fence, and he'd pace over there anxiously. This happened over and over again.

The people disappeared, and Mitchell focused on the Mustang before him. The creature was stunning with a dark coat and three black stockings. His hair was long ebony across his back with a thick tail. That muscle in his legs and shoulders was immense, and he clearly had a lot of power. It made him all the more beautiful.

Mitchell knew he had the tendency to see more in horses than in people. But with good reason, for the latter tended to be judgmental liars and hypocrites. On the other hand, a horse was constant and they were steady.

Most of his life was spent focusing on the care of horses and helping to capture and break them in gently. He'd done it on several of the drives, and that's how he'd found his current Appaloosa, Rascal. And the best part was that none of them judged him on his looks and besides this moment, were never scared of him.

Now he worked on this, helping the horse to recognize his voice so he understood he was not facing a threat. It was important to become friends first, Mitchell knew, and become familiar before trying anything. A whip only invited more fear and more anger, and those never boded well in these instances.

"That's right, boy, that's right. You just take it easy and we're going to say hello whenever you're ready. Maybe not now, maybe not today. We're going to do it your way, but it will happen. It's all on you and all up to you, so don't you worry about me. Just take it easy, and you can calm yourself down. There's no need to worry. They're not going to touch you."

The horse bucked, but he held his ground. Standing there, Mitchell tried to catch the horse's eyes. He shook his head several times and Mitchell stopped walking towards him, letting the animal test his limits. It got to the point that they followed each other nearly around the entire pen, but the horse stopped once he was between the crowd of people outside the fence and Mitchell. Stuck in the middle, the Mustang wasn't sure which one was worse, and waited with his legs shaking.

"It's all right," Mitchell murmured and crept forward. Only now he reached into a pocket and pulled out half of a carrot. He waved it slightly in the air so the Mustang could get the scent, and then set it on top of a post before stepping back.

Hands down, he waited. Waving his head about, the Mustang slowly stepped forward, and reached out for the carrot. After two attempts, he got it and started to eat. He would be distracted enough then, and Mitchell stepped forward just within arm's reach.

"See?" He offered with a small grin. "That wasn't so bad. No need to worry, boy." Once the horse finished eating, Mitchell put out his hands again and the horse didn't shy away this time. Instead, he sniffed for more snacks. Although there was nothing left, it helped the animal become familiar with his scent.

Within minutes he was gingerly brushing his hands across the Mustang. He heard a wallop of cheers and glanced towards the men from the corner of his eye. There were more of them there, he realized, and frowned at the noise. If they weren't careful, they'd spook the horse all over again. "Sorry about them," Mitchell mumbled. "They can be pretty dumb. But you, you're a beauty. Don't you forget that."

The horse was calm now so he climbed back onto the other side of the pen. By that point, several of the men had departed. "There he is," Mr. Connor chuckled and came over to Mitchell with an outstretched hand. "Boy, was that something! Have you had a lot of experience with horses?"

Nodding, Mitchell returned the firm handshake. "Yes, sir. They deserve proper attention and care, like we all do. If we want to work with them, we need to show them respect and patience."

"I like that." Matthew nodded thoughtfully. "I have a feeling you'd get along well with the Jessups. Have you met them?"

Glancing around at the men, Mitchell could feel their

eyes on him. He recognized the prick on the back of his neck, and he shifted his shoulders. Keeping his head down, the man fixed his collar higher and told himself it was nothing. He looked to Matthew, wondering if he had felt it, too. "I'm afraid I haven't had time to meet anyone in town yet."

That made the man grin. "Perfect. I'm taking them a pie. You're not busy, are you?"

He shrugged. "You're the boss, Boss."

Chapter Six

Christina

Most of it was white, the scenery outside the window of her seat on the train. White, with glimpses of blue sky. Christina's eyes were glued to it, squinting out at the world in the early morning and late nights on the train ride west. The journey was tiring, but she could hardly sleep.

She couldn't tell what it was, for the ache between her shoulder blades was more than just the strain of the stares she could feel on her back. After all, there was too much hair to hide beneath a bonnet, and there was no way to disguise her unusual features. There were whispers from all sides and the conductor wandered by her more often than she thought was appropriate.

It was more than just leaving her late parents behind along with her surviving aunt and uncle. And this went beyond her leaving the only home she had ever known. It was the fact that she was going somewhere new, strange, and unfamiliar. Just the thought of it made her heart hammer and her palms sweat.

Exhausted, she nearly missed her stop. Grabbing her bag, she struggled to join the others as they all stepped off the train. With a deep breath, she looked around to try to get her bearings. She could hardly keep her eyes open as she staggered off down the steps and into the street.

Christina noticed the buildings and the many people bustling about there. In Virginia, folks had a tendency of trying to stay indoors as much as possible. But here in Colorado, everyone acted as though it were summer the way the children played in the streets and women enjoyed a slow stroll without direction. It fascinated her, and she nearly missed the tall gentleman on his cart.

"Good day," he called, stopping just to the side so he didn't block her from the street.

Clutching her bag, she looked up and squinted. "Good day, sir."

He tipped his hat and glanced around at the street as she had. "Welcome to Rocky Ridge. I'm the sheriff in these hereabouts. Can I help you get wherever it is you need to go? Someone you might be here to see?"

Rubbing her face, she nodded hesitantly. Christina stepped a little closer but glanced at the street and realized it could always be a trap. She was innately wary because of her heritage and her past.

What would these folks be like? There was no telling, and she kept waiting for something to happen. The man seemed nice enough, but she still didn't know what to expect since she was a new face in town, and different. It wouldn't be the first time someone wanted her in jail for how she looked. "Possibly. Can you please direct me to the boarding house? It should be owned by the Jessups, and I'm not certain of which direction to go to get there."

Just as she was building up her resolve to walk as far as it took to get there rather than trust a stranger, the man chuckled. He was older than her by a few years and had a faded scar on one side of his face plus others she could see across the hands holding the reins. His smile caught her by surprise. And when he jumped down and put out a hand she fought the urge to bolt.

Stepping back, she held her purse tighter, ready to run if it came to that. "What is it?" She asked warily.

"Lucas Jessup at your service." He tipped his hat. "I pass by here often in case this happens. A woman coming for the boarding house." He shared the information as she remained tense and on guard. "Susannah, my sweet wife, will be glad to have another woman in the house, and I was about to head home. Would you like to join me?"

Weighing her options, Christina slowly nodded. After all there was still no reason to disbelieve him. She glanced at the cart that was filled with a few more goods. "Well, I suppose. I would appreciate that. Thank you, sir." Gingerly she handed over her bag and he set it carefully into the back of the cart.

She followed, turning to climb in to the back beside her bag. "Oh, please. You should ride up front. Here, let me help you up." Mr. Jessup pulled off his hat revealing a head of thick dark hair and beckoned her over.

Hesitantly, Christina glanced at the back. She always sat there, from habit and from never having enough space in the front. It was her aunt and uncle's seat, after all. Biting her lip, she tried to shrug off the unease and gave in to his request. He accepted her hand without shuddering and gave her the support she needed to sit on the front bench.

Mr. Jessup made it back around to his side and picked up the reins. "All right. Lemondrop, let's go home." He clicked his tongue and they started down the street. Clutching the board beneath her, Christina's breath caught as she felt the wind through her hair. She didn't get that in the back of a cart.

It became a rocking motion, one that made the tension in her shoulders fade away. All that was left, however, was her exhaustion. Her energy was used up in staying upright, with her eyes drifting closed until she felt a light hand on her shoulder.

Stirring, Christina rubbed her eyes. "Hmm?"

"We're here," Mr. Jessup told her softly, and then climbed down. Trying to hide her yawn, Christina glanced around to find herself in a barn. It was a very spacious one with a loft and several stalls. The man was putting the horse he called Lemondrop into one of the stalls. After that, he came over to her side with a kind grin. "Are you ready to come down?"

Blushing, she nodded and accepted his outstretched hand. "Yes, of course. I apologize, I didn't realize we were here." When she reached the ground, she wavered and put a hand on the wagon for support as he handed over her bag.

"The house is this way," he offered politely, and guided her towards the house. She stumbled several times but managed to stay upright. Her vision blurred but she focused on the door, which Mr. Jessup opened for them. "Susie darling," he called out. "We have a guest!"

He started putting away the items he had carried

inside, and she stood nervously by the door. Though she tried to concentrate on staying alert, Christina's resolve was fading just as a bright ball of energy came into the kitchen. "A guest? Oh, hello. Welcome! My name is Susannah Jessup. Lucas, how long have you two been here? I didn't know we were expecting anyone. But never mind that, our door is always open and we're very, very glad to have you, dear." She looked warmly at Christina and took a step closer.

The woman was petite, around the same height, with long blonde hair and bright blue eyes. While they shared several similar qualities, Mrs. Jessup was much paler with much lighter hair and eyes. She had the biggest smile and clasped her hands together for just a moment before wrapping Christina in a firm hug. "Thank you," Christina managed, blinking several times, and then covered a big yawn with her hand. "Oh, I'm terribly sorry. It was a long trip."

She shook her head, yellow curls bouncing. "If you're from back east, I'm sure it was! What's your name, dear?"

"Christina Bristol." Another yawn escaped.

The other woman tutted. "You've had a long journey, indeed. Where do you hail from, dear? Can I get you any water?" Then she started getting one before Christina could say anything.

"Virginia," Christina said finally. She glanced at the ground, feeling their gazes on her, but she wasn't sure she wanted to offer all the details.

There was a moment of silence before Susannah returned and handed her a glass of water. "I suppose we can save conversation for later. You look weary, so let's get you to your room so you can rest. Come with me and I'll help you settle in. I'm assuming you came here for the boarding house, is that right?"

Christina nodded, and glanced back at the kitchen as they left. Still clutching her bag, she trailed after the blonde woman. Mrs. Jessup had a dancing gait, and she wondered how the woman had so much life to her. She focused on the swirls of blonde hair as she was led to a room. It was lovely with a soft bed and softer blankets. There was a window with lace curtains, and a chest for her things.

"Here we are," Susannah proclaimed proudly. "You can call this yours while you're here. Welcome. I'm pleased to have you here with us, dear."

"Thank you, ma'am. Mrs. Jessup, I mean."

"You're here to learn the skills and find yourself a husband, yes?" The words came out awkwardly as they glanced at one another. "I just want to make sure there's no misunderstanding about that part of what we do here."

There it was, put in its plainest terms. Christina hesitated, unable to meet her gaze as she nodded. "Yes, ma'am." She blushed deeply as she agreed. Though she believed this is what she needed to do, the whole thing was a little embarrassing.

The woman bit her lip. "And there were no suitors back home?" she pressed. "I don't mean to ask much, of course, I shouldn't be—well, Lucas tells me I pry too much so I apologize if that's rude. I just want to be clear that you're unmarried and looking to change that."

Shrugging, Christina leaned against the bedpost. "I am, yes."

Susannah appeared to sigh in relief, but Christina

couldn't be sure. It was taking more strength to keep her eyes open than to stand.

"I understand. Well, you should get some rest, dear. I'll come back later to get you for supper in case you're hungry. We'll be in the main house if you need anything. Sleep well." She waved and closed the door behind her.

By that point, her mind was no longer able to function. It took all of Christina's strength to pull off her shoes and put her bag down on the chest. She was halfway under the bundle of blankets when her eyes closed, and she immediately fell asleep.

Chapter Seven

Susannah

"I had to be positive that she was actually here to be a mail-order bride," Susannah explained as she set the utensils around the table carefully. "So I wasn't prying. I just wanted to be sure. We all need to be very, very clear about what is going on here. Um, I need to be, is the best way to say that, I suppose. I must make sure that each young woman is here to start a new life. To find a husband. And I think that's important. Don't you?"

Lucas was at the other end of the table and she watched his brow furrow in concentration, torn between the conversation and reviewing their accounts. "I suppose. But I saw her face when she didn't say where she was from."

"She answered. She said Virginia."

"And you were about to pry. You had your prying face on," Lucas told her, not even looking her way. It bugged her. Pouting, Susannah set the last of the silverware down and put her hands on her hips. Then she stared at him until he sighed, giving her an exasperated look in response. "Susie darling, you meant well, I know. I'm just saying that she was past the point of exhaustion. All that could have waited."

After a minute, Susannah let it go. "All right, fine. The poor thing was certainly tired. But oh, she's lovely. Isn't she? That hair, it looks like pure silk. I've never seen anything like it. That young lady is a remarkable one, I just know it." Susannah beamed and went over, rubbing his shoulder. "I have a good feeling about her, don't you?"

Several of the papers slipped from his hands and he made a face. But he left them there, taking a deep breath before looking at her. With a soft smile, Lucas took her hand in his and pulled her onto his lap. Her breath caught at the swift movement and raised she her eyebrows at him. "Everything turns out well when you're around," he said finally, and tugged on her hair lovingly.

Smiling, Susannah leaned forward and gently touched his cheek. Already there was scruff across his chin and she could feel the unevenness of his old scar. Lucas's features were so familiar to her that she didn't even need her eyes to know it was him. His scent, his voice, his touch. Everything about him was unique, and she knew every wrinkle and breath. "Only because you're my luck," she chuckled. "Now, is that pumpkin I smell?"

"I hope so." He kissed her nose. "Because I'm starving." His stomach agreed by groaning loudly. It made Susannah laugh, and she hopped off his lap. After they blessed the food, Susannah took a plate down to the young woman's room, but when she peeked in, the girl was fast asleep.

He didn't have much to say about their journey from

town, only that Miss Christina Bristol was quiet and uncomfortable but that was to be expected. Susannah cleaned the kitchen and they gathered blankets with a book to read out on the porch. Lucas fixed the lantern on the table and wrapped an arm around her.

"We don't do this often enough." She sighed happily, leaning against him as her heart pattered lightly inside her chest when he started the story.

Lucas was only in two chapters when his speech slowed down. Immediately she looked up and realized he was looking ahead. Straightening up, Susannah found a wagon headed in their direction. It was small but they were close enough for her to recognize it. "It's the Connors!"

Sure enough, Matthew pulled up at the gate. At first she had supposed that the figure beside him would be his wife, but Eleanor was much slighter. And they weren't in a hurry, so that meant nothing was wrong. Lucas moved to the edge of the stairs, welcoming the men.

"Hello." He tipped his hat with a grin. "I'm Lucas Jessup," he added to the unfamiliar figure.

It was another man, more roughly dressed than Matthew. He was tall, thick with muscle, and though he offered a polite smile, he was more than ready to keep his head low and the hat on.

"This is Mitchell Powell," Matthew explained, and took the package from him. "We bring you a pie! Eleanor requested I bring it to you immediately. Then I brought Mitch along for company."

Though Susannah accepted the pie, Lucas was right there hovering over her to peek through and sniff at what it might be. With one deep inhale, he grinned down at her. "It's huckleberry."

His expression made her chuckle. "Then I suppose we had best dish it out now, shouldn't we? Gentlemen, would you like to join us inside?"

Matthew shook his head. "No, that's all right. We don't want our dirty boots on your clean floors. But I wouldn't say no to a piece of pie," he added with a wink.

Laughing, she nodded. "Perfect. I'll be back in a moment and bring some cider to go with it." Humming, she stepped inside to gather everything. Moving quickly about, she was able to load everything up in one trip back to the men. The tray was heavy and Lucas was quick to grab it from her once she reached the door. Susannah passed around the plates and mugs before sitting back on the bench with her husband. They nodded their thanks and all bit into the delicious treat. It was perfect, as all of Eleanor's huckleberry pies were since she'd perfected the recipe.

Susannah eyed the men curiously as they ate their pie, and she looked at the stranger again. If Matthew liked him, then he had to be a good man and that was enough for her. "Mr. Powell," she called him out, watching him keep his head hunched and his collar up. Cocking her head, she tried to catch a better glimpse of the man. When he heard his name, his eyes lifted and met hers. Only then did she realize why he kept his face hidden.

On the right side of Mitchell's face was what appeared to be a birthmark. It was a little darker than the rest of his face and covered about half of his cheek. It made sense then, and her heart went out to him. Everything he did was to maneuver that mark out of ev-

eryone's sight. But she was undeterred, for her own
husband wore a scar of his own. Susannah smiled when
their eyes met.

"Have you been in Rocky Ridge long?" She smiled
and waited on his response.

Glancing around, he shook his head. "No, ma'am,
I haven't."

"Well, welcome!" She beamed. "We're glad to have
you here. The Connors are wonderful folks, and I'm
sure you'll settle in quite nicely."

Mitchell cleared his throat. "I hope so. Yes, thank
you."

Finished with his pie, Lucas settled back with an arm
around his wife. She appreciated the extra warmth and
grinned at him, offering him a bite of her pie which he
eagerly took. She chuckled. "Matthew, how is the ranch
these days? And the girls?"

Swallowing the last of his cider, Matthew Connor
relaxed back in his own chair. "Good, and wonderful.
Eleanor wants you two to join us for supper soon. Our
little one is going through teething pains, but perhaps
next month would be good?"

Nodding, Susannah glanced at her husband. "Yes,
of course. Hopefully when the snow melts we'll be able
to gather together more often. The drive here wasn't
difficult?"

"Not at all," he assured them. "It's been a lovely
week. Oh, and I don't think we told you, but our next
herd of horses just arrived. They are exquisite, Susannah. Lucas, if you're needing any horses, be sure to
let me know. Once they're broken, they'll be great for
whatever you need."

Lucas nodded, stealing another bite of Susannah's

pie. "I'll think about it, thank you. And Powell, what are you doing? Are you working with the horses?"

For some reason, Matthew chuckled. He glanced at the man before nodding to the Jessups. "He sure is. Mitchell managed to get a Mustang eating right out of his hand this very afternoon."

Susannah glanced at her husband who would understand this statement better, knowing very little of horses herself. Just the idea made her squirm in her seat. But Lucas squeezed her tight in her discomfort and nodded to the gentlemen. "That's very impressive. Have you worked with horses often?"

The young gentleman shrugged, running a hand through his dark hair before setting the hat snugly back in place. "On and off, I suppose. I just think that I understand them, that's all. They're good creatures, with good hearts."

Matthew grinned proudly. "He has a way with them, that's for certain. Now, enough about us. How are things with you? And the boarding house?"

Setting down her empty plate, Susannah wrapped her shawl more tightly around her shoulders. "Things are very well. Lucas repaired a broken horseshoe, and we're going to have a few calves due in a few months, it looks like. And just today we had a young lady arrive," she added with a bright grin. "Oh, she is darling. Her name is Miss Christina Bristol and I'm sure you'll see her around town soon."

"Lovely." Matthew nodded, and turned to Mitchell. "The Jessups run a boarding house for women. Actually, Susannah is a matchmaker. Women come stay here as long as they need to and learn valuable skills. And she introduces them to gentlemen she thinks would be a good match. She has marvelous insight and she's quite successful."

Susannah shook her head with pink tinged cheeks. "You're too kind, Matthew. It takes a lot of hard work for everyone to make things happen. I just want to be there to help women settle out here."

"How do you match them up?" Mitchell cocked his head curiously. "What happens if they, well, they don't like each other?"

"The moment things aren't going well, we bring it to a stop. We've had a few slip ups along the way, but so far everything has concluded happily. I want the very best for everyone. You see—" she paused as she met his gaze again "—I came out west to marry Lucas and knew very little about how to run a household here. I know other women are coming out to take this same journey. Now they can come here to learn skills and they help with my duties and I'm able to help them find husbands."

Mitchell shrugged. "Who are the husbands? Just strangers?"

She shook her head adamantly. "My clients are good men that come with references from other good people. I build portfolios and sort through the files to see who might work well with one another. There are certain commonalities between folks, and we all have certain needs. And we've been very blessed, as have the women who have come our way. Like I said, it's a lot of hard work, but every woman here has found a husband. If you're able to explore town, you might be able to meet a few of the couples."

Clearing his throat, Matthew pointed to himself. "We didn't pay for her services, but she definitely tested her talents on us. Eleanor grew up with Susannah in Boston and came out here to visit. A long story short, she never returned to Boston." He chuckled and leaned back. "And I'm grateful for that every day."

Susannah beamed and glanced at Mitchell whose gaze had dropped again, and she worried they had talked too much. They'd had his attention just a moment ago, but what changed? He was an interesting man, she decided, and couldn't help but wonder what his story was. The topic soon changed and he hardly said another word before it was time for them to leave.

Chapter Eight

Christina

Morning came, and the sunlight woke her from a deep sleep. After rubbing her eyes, Christina sat up and looked around at her surroundings. It took her a minute to remember where she was, that she wasn't at home anymore. She was in a strange room, a new and unfamiliar place.

Colorado. She had left Virginia. The emotions of the last few weeks returned just like that, and she didn't know what to do about it. Inhaling deeply, Christina gripped the blankets and convinced herself to climb out of bed. She was here, and she had to get on with her life. Maybe by going to work she could sort those thoughts out.

And that's what she did.

"Good morning," she sang out after dressing for the day and finding her way to the kitchen. The woman, Mrs. Jessup, turned from the cupboards and beamed. Rubbing her hands together, Christina tried to take it all in. "How can I help?"

For a week, she started to get the run of things. They had early breakfasts, she helped with the cows, and handled the laundry. There was gardening, too, that reminded her of her uncle's farm in Virginia. There were moments where it felt like nothing had changed. Christina loved slipping her fingers into the moist dirt, and rubbing soft leaves against her cheek. The ground was fresh and tender, growing everything they needed to survive. It was something familiar for Christina, reminding her of her family.

That was a bittersweet realization, as she glanced at the winter garden. Her mother had loved the winter garden. Suddenly, she missed the kind woman who had raised her, and held her in her arms whenever she needed comfort. Her mother, who smelled like chestnuts and always had a song to hum and had those twinkling blue eyes. The only person that Christina could trust would never hurt her and would always love her.

And she wasn't there. And she wouldn't be ever again.

Though she'd cried a thousand tears already, the pain was still there in her heart. A tear escaped before she could help herself. It hit her all over again like a crashing wave and she curled her hands into fists, trying to stay in control. Bowing her head, she tried to hide the tears behind a curtain of hair. A lump formed in her throat.

Behind her, Christina heard the porch door swing open, then slam closed. She jumped and hurriedly wiped away the tears that were beginning to trickle down her cheeks. Sniffling, the young woman frantically grabbed at the pile of weeds before her, trying to remember what she was doing just a minute ago. In her haste, she mixed up the weeds and threw several over by the peas, and scrambled to rectify her mistake before that was noticed.

"Still out here, are you?" Mrs. Jessup hummed cheerfully, coming up to her side. "Well, isn't this a marvelous sight. You truly are a wonder to behold. I think my cabbage heads have doubled their size since you arrived."

As she knelt to join her, Christina hurriedly scooted over to make room while keeping her head down. Her heart pounded as she tried to remain inconspicuous—this was what she was used to. Being in a new place with new people didn't change that. "Oh my. Um, I suppose…well, it's just the sun in my eyes," she stammered, trying to keep her voice from breaking. Taking a deep breath, she tried to pull herself together. But her chin wobbled, and a tear dripped off and splattered into the dirt.

Susannah started to chuckle, but it died away and Christina knew she had been found out. The woman breathed out softly, slipping a delicate white finger between the curtain of black hair, just enough for their eyes to meet. Christina tried to look away, but the tears sprung back. "Oh dear," Susannah murmured sympathetically. "Oh, it's all right. Whatever the matter is, it will be just fine."

She wrapped her arms around Christina and pulled her close as if they were old friends. It only brought back the memories of her mother more, and Christina couldn't hide it any longer. She tried to say something only to choke on her voice as the woman squeezed her tightly. "Oh, dear. I'm sorry," Christina stammered. "I just miss her. I didn't expect it to be so painful right now."

"Shh." Susannah brushed her fingers through her hair, still clean and tender. The soothing motions helped Christina to gather her breath again, swallowing the lump in her throat. The pain in her chest was still there, but it was manageable and she could breathe again. "Whatever it is," Susannah continued to murmur, "everything will be just fine. You're going to be well, Christina, all is going to be well."

Hiccupping, Christina finally pulled back, and fumbled for a handkerchief from her pockets with shaking hands. Susannah brushed the girl's hair away from her face, and kept a comforting hand on her as she wiped away her tears. "I'm terribly sorry," Christina murmured, swallowing hard again. "I didn't mean to be so weak."

Mrs. Jessup shook her head. "You're not weak at all! It's a hard thing, leaving everything you know. Leaving the life you had behind can be quite painful, good or bad. If you really need to, dear, we'll help you get back home. If you decide this isn't really your best path, we'll understand."

It was a kind offer. Christina shook her head miserably. "There is no home for me back in Virginia, ma'am. I lost my mother not long before this. She's the one who wanted me to leave Virginia to make a new start. It's just hard. She was such a good mother and she was always there for me. Now I don't quite know what I'm supposed to do. Have you ever felt lost?"

Susannah nodded and squeezed her hand. "Yes. Yes, I have. We all face our own trials at one point or another. But dear, it doesn't mean you need to go through this alone. And it doesn't mean you'll be stuck in this place forever." She offered a sympathetic smile, and glanced around. "Come, let's get you washed up and fed, shall we? Some food in the belly always helps. And perhaps you can tell me more about your lovely mother."

Staggering to her feet, Christina nodded and glanced at her dirty hands. There was mud on Susannah's dress, but when she mentioned it, the blonde only chuckled and idly brushed at it as she led the way into the house. Lucas was already seated at the table, having stayed home for the day to leave his deputy on the job. He glanced at the women but said nothing as he carefully continued slicing the fresh loaf of bread.

"There's nothing better than a good slice of bread," Susannah announced decidedly. "Lucas, fetch the butter, would you? There's a new batch right next to the milk. I'll pull the chicken off the fire and we'll have a lovely meal."

Christina was grateful for their kindness, the comfort and the willingness to look beyond the tears. She was ashamed of her childish actions and kept her head low as she ate, not very hungry and just picking at her food. Part of her just kept waiting for one of them to tell her she was being foolish, yet nothing like that happened. After a few minutes of staring at her food, she knew there was no way she could finish it. The delicious scent just wasn't enough for her queasy stomach.

Just as Susannah was finishing off her coffee, Lucas suddenly paused as he held his nearly finished sandwich in both hands. His eyes focused on the vacant space ahead of him before he finally turned around, facing the front door. "It sounds like Matthew's cart," he announced a moment later. Christina still hadn't heard a thing and watched as the man finished his food in two bites, nodded to the ladies, and headed for the door.

"Yes," Susannah said after a moment, and looked at her with a knowing half-smile. "He's always like that." The woman opened her mouth to say something else but dropped her gaze to Christina's plate. She'd only managed a few bites. Just as Christina was preparing to apologize, the blonde stood up. "Let's get you some cider, shall we? Perhaps that will ease your stomach. Are you comfortable there?"

In the distance, the front door opened and there were more voices. Christina's throat constricted as she glanced down at her hands, several shades darker than Susannah's. And her nearly black long hair was a clear marker as well. Though she still hadn't been to town since her arrival, she worried that the people there might be just like the people in Virginia. Standing up, she glanced around at the kitchen. The voices sounded closer. "I, well actually, I think… I think some fresh air might do me well."

Mrs. Jessup glanced up from the kettle and brought her a warm mug. "Don't forget a shawl, then. I'll join you, if you like, after I see to the gentlemen." She opened the door for Christina and disappeared back inside. "Good afternoon! It's lovely to see you. Can I get you some cider, perhaps, or coffee?"

The door closed behind her and Christina was alone. That sensation of aggravated nerves slowly deflated as she looked around and leaned against the post looking out. It was the back porch facing the mountains, and they appeared to go on forever. Green and brown and white on top, a beautiful blur. It was the only good thing about Virginia, the land and those mountains. Christina breathed more easily then at the comforting sight and sipped her cider.

A step creaked and she turned, nearly spilling her drink. Coming up from the side porch, a man appeared. One hand on the rail, the stranger stopped as their gazes met, both realizing they weren't alone. Christina clenched her cup tightly, and inhaled deeply. His eyes were as blue as ice and for a minute that's all she could see.

Chapter Nine

 ❧

Mitchell

It was a lovely day, and Mitchell had intended to use it working with the horses. Some of the men were already beginning to act like most people, ignoring him or leaving extra work on his hands. It happened often enough, so he kept to himself and stuck with the horses. However, he had experience in areas that Matthew did and the man came to him daily with questions and ideas.

The current idea was about building a large stable in a new section of the Connor's expanding ranch. For the last two days, the two of them had been drawing up some plans but Matthew wasn't certain what sort of structure he wanted to use for groundwork in case of bad weather. For this reason, the two men had packed up their plans and brought them over to the Jessups' house for Lucas's input.

Not only was he the town's sheriff, but Lucas Jessup helped with most town plans for building and construction. Most of the buildings in Rocky Ridge as well as Colorado Springs had once been worked on by the man, and Matthew trusted him to steer them in the right direction. After being welcomed inside and handed a warm cup of coffee, Mitchell glanced at the two men who were already lost in conversation without him.

Excusing himself, he stepped outside. It was a good day with only a few clouds in the sky. There hadn't been fresh snow lately and Mitchell knew they needed to take advantage of that. After he gulped his coffee, he left the mug on the front bench and started to wander around. It was a magnificent place cradled by the mountains. But it was far enough, he noticed, just enough that an avalanche wouldn't hit them. The Jessups' home was snug, spacious, and far enough outside of town that they wouldn't be bothered.

He was impressed. Trailing his hands along the smooth oak, he made his way around the house on the wrap-around porch with his eyes wandering. The windows were framed with lace, a woman's touch. The porch was just wide enough for two folks to walk together, and the roof didn't block any of the view.

So lost in the mountains beyond, Mitchell didn't realize anyone else was around until he noticed the figure standing by a post. In the same moment, he stepped on a plank that squeaked, and he knew he was caught. There was a twirl of skirts and dark hair as another set of eyes met his. They were so dark that he thought he was drowning in them. He tried to swallow but couldn't find his tongue.

The two of them stood there for a minute, staring at one another. Until all at once, they both managed to break the spell and looked away. Mitchell glanced down at his boots, stepping on the squeaking plank again. The man winced. Clearing his throat, he gripped the railing again and considering turning back, but if he said nothing that would be perceived as rude.

"My apologies," he offered hesitantly. "I, um… I thought I was…that is, I didn't know there was anyone else out here. On the porch, I mean."

She moved back as he stepped forward. Mitchell stopped, wondering if it was because of him but the woman was moving further back, helping him realize that she was just making room for him. Swallowing, the young man joined her there, hand still trailing across the railings hesitantly.

"It's all right," she said softly. "Did you come for the Jessups?"

Mitchell shrugged and swallowed. "More or less. I work for the Connors on their ranch, and Matthew wanted to speak with Lucas. He's building another stable, you see. And he wanted Mr. Jessup's eyes on it. They didn't really need me," he added after a moment. Fingers drumming on the wood, he glanced around. She knew where the best view was, and it made him grin. The view was spectacular—all the way up the mountains.

"Do you like it? Your job, I mean." She cut her eyes away quickly and her voice was low. She fiddled with her mug, and he could feel her gaze on him a few moments later.

Glancing over, Mitchell fixed his hat and tried to sneak a better glance at her. With a small adjustment to his collar, he was certain she couldn't see his birthmark as he looked.

She had hair darker than midnight that hung in a braid almost to her waist, though a few wisps draped around her cheeks. Even from that angle he saw her

long sloping nose and high cheekbones. Her skin was
smooth and rich, reminding him of the Apache war-
riors he'd spent a winter holed up with. Whoever she
was, the young lady was more beautiful than anyone he
had ever seen. His heart hammered and made his face
flush as he remembered she had asked him a question.
The woman turned to him, waiting.

"I do, yes." He nodded quickly and smiled at her. The
woman's eyes were open and for some reason she was
easy to talk to. "I've been looking to settle down and
working with the Connors on their ranch has been very
good for me. They're letting me work with the horses,
you see, and breaking them in."

She bit her lip. "That sounds dangerous."

Without thinking about it, Mitchell took a few steps
closer and shrugged. "Only if you don't know what
you're doing. Only those who don't understand the animals need to be afraid of them. Horses are like humans,
and you have to treat them with respect. That's the trick.
If you can do that, then those creatures will respect you
back. And there you have it. Simple but true."

"It's that easy?"

He chuckled at her raised eyebrow. "Well, I suppose there's a few other tricks involved. But once you
do that, the work gets much easier. It's been a week and
already I've been riding a Mustang that wouldn't allow
anyone near him. One of the boys, Kyle, has been calling him Thunder. The horse is young, and he's got a lot
of spirit. That's all."

Nodding, she cocked her head at him. There was a
hint of a smile there, in the corners of her lips. "Spirit
is good," she said at last. "I'm sure Thunder appreci-
ates your respect. I can see that you really like horses."

Mitchell shrugged and glanced away for a moment. "They've been better to me than most people." Realizing he'd said that aloud, he cleared his throat. "Meaning that animals aren't as complicated as we are, I mean. I'm not saying that people are bad, and horses are all I care about. Just a little easier to talk to. For me, anyway." Biting his tongue, Mitchell wished he could stop talking.

But the problem was, he enjoyed talking with her. "I like that," she said thoughtfully. "They don't judge you or lie to you. They are who they are, and they don't mind who you are. I'm only sorry I haven't thought of that before. I would have made friends with all the horses I ever met had I known this."

She was holding back a laugh, he knew it. But it wasn't a cruel one. Mitchell glanced after her as she looked up at the mountain and then turned and sat down on the bench. He glanced back at her and she smiled.

"My name is Christina, by the way. Christina Bristol."

Tipping his hat, Mitchell offered an elaborate grin. "Mitchell Powell at your service. It's a pleasure to meet you, Miss Bristol. You know my business, then, and what I'm doing here at the Jessups' place. Are you a friend of Miss Susannah's?"

"I'd like to think so." She glanced down at her empty cup, and set it aside to shift her shawl higher onto her shoulders. It was chilly for a bright day and he felt a chill, too. Mitchell noticed the empty spot on the bench beside her and he considered trying to sit beside her. He took another step forward but hesitated as she sighed. "I've come to Rocky Ridge to get away from Virginia. I'm just looking for something new, you could say. Perhaps I'll start breaking in horses."

A laugh escaped his lips before he could help it. "You should," he offered. "I'll teach you everything I know. Are you enjoying Colorado?"

As she started speaking, a thought occurred to Mitchell. She was talking about how Colorado was better than Virginia, and last week came to his mind. Her name had sounded familiar for a reason. It had been his first visit here to the Jessups' since Matthew wanted to drop off that pie. He hadn't known what to do and was quiet for most of the conversation, though they had brought up the boarding house.

Mrs. Jessup housed young ladies who came to Rocky Ridge looking to start new lives. And to find suitors. Mitchell bit his tongue again as he realized that Miss Bristol was who Mrs. Jessup had mentioned, about a young lady who had just arrived. She had mentioned the young woman was lovely, but there was no way he would have imagined she was this stunning.

They talked for a few more minutes, for she was friendly and sweet. Conversation was easy between them, and he enjoyed their conversation. Mitchell began to step closer the more they talked, until he was leaning against the post. He was just in the middle of telling his story about getting lost in the middle of Tennessee during an unexpected blizzard when he glanced down at his hands where he was playing with his hat.

The hat he used to hide his birthmark. Blood drained from his face, realizing that the mark would be out in daylight then, right in front of this beautiful woman. Trailing off, he couldn't recall the end of his story. Straightening up, Mitchell hastily turned away. "Anyway, I ended up meeting some Apache and they helped me. But it's not an interesting story, I'm afraid. I guess I should go."

She stood in surprise. "Go?"

He stepped back in a hurry, bumping into the railing. Mitchell grabbed it to steady himself, and shot one last glance, wondering if Christina Bristol had seen it, if she had noticed his clumsiness or his birthmark. Ransacking his mind, he ran through their conversation. Was there a moment where she had moved, or paused? She must have noticed, she must have seen his terrible imperfection. "I need to go get that cup I left in front." Shoving the hat on his head, he turned and strode away with quick steps. "I have to go."

"Farewell, then."

He barely heard her since he'd started walking away before his last words were out of his mouth. Mitchell could feel the heat climbing up his face and that only frustrated him more. That ruined everything, that horrid mark of his. Children cried, women couldn't look at him, and men tried to hide their curiosity. It was always the same. Everyone was the same in the end, so what had he been doing? There was no reason to suspect Miss Bristol would be any different than the others.

Bitterness swept over him as he returned to the front of the house and picked up the cup. He entered the kitchen but hung back in the shadows as Matthew and Lucas talked. His eyes swept over the back door a couple of times, certain he could see Miss Bristol there. But she never came inside, and he was grateful for it. He couldn't face her again.

Soon their business at the Jessups' was done and they were headed back to the ranch, a place where he was judged for his work and not his looks. He was comfortable there and was thankful for the opportunity Matthew had given him.

Chapter Ten

Susannah

The area in the corner where the desk was located filled with natural light from the morning sun. Clouds were on their way in so Susannah was taking advantage of the good weather before it went away. Humming, she sat at the desk and sorted through her files. But the frowning started and grew deeper imprints on her cheeks as she looked through more of them.

"I'm back." Her husband's smiling face appeared at her side after he'd silently crept up on her. Susannah jumped in surprise, nearly dropping everything in her arms. "Is something wrong?" he added, choosing not to laugh this time at surprising her. He did it nearly every day, but still found amusement in it.

Sighing, she pushed everything back onto the table and raised a hand flippantly. "Well, nothing is really wrong, but it's also not right. I've been looking over possible matches for Christina, and nothing appears to be turning up."

Stepping through the doorway, Lucas glanced around

at the scattered files and skimmed through a few of them himself. "There are several gentlemen here I know who have spoken with you. They can't have all disappeared, can they?"

"These three have since found wives." She picked up a few folders and then another two. "And these ones have left for California. I have these two, but they never finished their profiles and I'm a little wary of them. They won't talk to me in town, either. And who am I missing? Let me see…no, no, and no." Slapping them back on the table, Susannah pouted. "I haven't had a decent client register since summer, Lucas. How am I supposed to find Christina a husband when I don't have anyone?"

He hesitated. "Is she desperate to find someone soon?"

She bit her lip, and tried to think. "She's settled in here very well. The girl is talented, especially in the garden and in the kitchen. She has quite the flair. Christina is lovely, Lucas, a beautiful woman who seems fairly happy here. I love having her here, you know this. But she's supposed to be finding a husband and I can't seem to find one for her. She deserves to find a good match."

He tilted his head to the side and shrugged.

Before he could add his thoughts, she continued. "I always sort of assumed my problem would be finding women," she admitted, "not the men. I haven't tried advertising to them since I had enough clients. We've already helped several out, and I'm simply not certain of what to do about this. Even if I do send advertisements to gentlemen, there's no telling how long it will take."

Lucas stared at the table thoughtfully for a moment. Susannah could see the wheels turning in his head as he tried to sort out an idea. Her heart pounded hopefully and she stood up, waiting. His eyes were bright and she could tell something was on his mind; if she was lucky then that something would help her out.

"Well?" she asked anxiously, unable to wait anymore. Hurrying around the table, she wrapped her arms around him. "Lucas?"

He raised an eyebrow looking down at her before wrapping his own arms around her waist. "If you must know," Lucas said after a moment, "that never helps me think more clearly. I get sidetracked." But he chuckled and kissed her forehead.

Beaming, Susannah kissed his cheek in return. "Please tell me you have an idea, Lucas."

"I was talking to Dr. Fitzgerald today, and he mentioned he was waiting on one of Eleanor's huckleberry pies. He said that he and his wife had ordered two weeks ago and still hadn't received one."

She frowned. "Is something wrong with Eleanor? She's never that slow. Did something happen to her berry bushes? Perhaps I should go see her."

"And take Christina," he hinted.

Susannah squinted up at him, trying to follow wherever his train of thought had led him. "Take Christina to meet Eleanor to help her make new friends?"

He chuckled and twirled her. "Susie darling, more than that. You want to keep her busy, don't you? It'll buy you some more time and keep her distracted. Eleanor receives some help, Christina makes a friend, and you have the time you need to look for a good suitor. Everybody wins."

It made sense. The more she thought about it, the better it sounded. Gasping, Susannah looked at him with a wide smile. "You're absolutely right! Why, that's brilliant, Lucas! I think she'll enjoy helping Eleanor and they'll both have a lot of fun. Oh, and she'll be able to meet the children. What are we waiting for?" Hurrying out of the study, she headed towards the door for her jacket and boots. "We just need Christina and she's around here somewhere. Stitching, I think. She'll like a break."

Lucas had trailed after her. "Aren't you forgetting something?"

She stopped, one arm in her jacket. Glancing about, she shrugged at him. "What are you talking about?"

He laughed and came over to her. As he took her coat away, Lucas directed her towards the window. In that short space of time, the clouds had already begun to cover up the sky and rain was beginning to fall. A short breath escaped her slouched shoulders. "Oh. Right." The storm they were expecting was arriving. That was the reason Lucas had only stopped into town for a few supplies to hold them over in case it was very bad.

"Next week," Lucas promised her. "Or once the road isn't so wet, I'll take you ladies down to the Connors' ranch. Eleanor can wait until then. And who knows? Perhaps you can try your hand at a few pies until then."

She suppressed an urge to roll her eyes and grinned. He wrapped his arms around her, resting his chin on top of her head as she continued looking outside. The sky was gray and looked like it would continue to darken. Biting her lip, she told herself not to be disappointed. It would have been a rash idea, just leaving like that to see the Connors anyway. Susannah felt herself begin to sway side to side with Lucas's pull and smiled. "Perhaps, dear, perhaps."

She grew distracted with the brewing storm. The animals needed to be cared for, and windows needed to be blocked. It was late by the time everything was safely tied down or put off the floor. After all these years, the Jessups had their storm preparation custom down perfectly. By the time the winds picked up, everyone was gathered around the fireplace with warm drinks and slices of apple cake.

Though the bad weather went on through the night, Lucas managed to get some rest. Susannah was restless and kept glancing through the slits near the window as though she might see something. Occasionally there was lightning, but otherwise the night was black. The wind whistled in her ears, and she hummed an old hymn from Boston.

It wasn't the terrible soaking they had anticipated, although it took them a few days to get the wagon out for a trip over the muddy road. The mud was just enough to be inconvenient. Finally on the third day, the sun came out bright and strong and dried the ground enough to make a trip to the Connors an easy journey.

"We're going out!" She sang out early that morning, finishing the eggs as Christina arrived to have breakfast. "Hurry up, and we'll need to be on our way. You'll want to dress warmly, of course. It's still chilly. We're going to the Connor ranch today. Oh, you're going to love them. They're the sweetest people, and have the loveliest ranch."

Christina offered a hesitant smile. "Will there be someone to stay here? I'd hate to leave the animals alone. Unprotected. Are you certain I should join you?"

Pausing, Susannah just stared at her, confused. "But of course, dear. You need friends here in Rocky Ridge. You've been here over a month and you haven't left our property. Don't you want to go out and meet people? Now we'll be going to church this Sunday and I hope you'll join us but until then, Eleanor Connor will be so happy to welcome you to our circle."

There was a small tug at her curved lips, a downward turn. What was that for? There was a dark look on the woman's face that was so short Susannah wondered if she was imagining things. Surely Christina was tired of being here with so little company. But the silence was more telling than her words.

Clearing her throat, Susannah thought quickly. Perhaps finding new friends wasn't the most important thing to her at the moment. "Eleanor is an old friend of mine, you see, and she's been swamped with orders for her pies lately. It happens around this time every year and there are more and more people who want them. Since you're so talented in the kitchen, I thought you might like to help her out. I'm certain she could use the assistance."

"All right." Christina nodded slowly, clearly unsure. But she looked less reluctant then. "I'd like to be of help, if I can." And they left it at that, though she noticed the younger woman barely touched her breakfast after it was decided that she'd help Eleanor out in the kitchen.

After the morning meal, the ladies pulled on their cloaks and set up the cart. It was a long drive but the sun was warm. Susannah sang for much of the way, and Christina even chimed in, blushing madly every time. Soon enough they were pulling up at the front of the ranch, and several of the boys ran to help them.

"It's good to see you all," Susannah called out. "I brought some cake. Make sure even those men in the barn get some, you hear? And where's Eleanor, is she inside?"

"Sure is," one of the boys chimed. "We'll get your horse taken care of, ma'am."

She beamed and he blushed, a tall skinny thing who was much younger than herself. Or at least, that's how it felt. "That's just swell of you! Thank you very much." Looping an arm through Christina's, they headed up to the house. The ladies only had to knock once before the door was opened for them.

"Susannah!" Eleanor enveloped her friend in a tight hug. "I wasn't expecting you, but I'm delighted you're here! Come in, come in. Please, pardon the mess. It's been so busy. There've been pies to make, you see, and then the storm slowed down the orders. Can you believe that? Then little Susie's had a fever, and she hasn't been sleeping. Oh, do come in, my apologies!" She spoke quickly, pulling them inside and helping them off with their coats.

Chuckling, Susannah pulled her into a second hug, a tight one where Eleanor couldn't do anything but was forced to slow down. "Then it's a good thing we're here," she assured her friend. "I've brought Miss Christina Bristol with me. She's come from Virginia and is staying at our boarding house. Christina, this is my dearest friend in all the world, Eleanor Connor."

"You've brought help?" Eleanor was so happy that she sniffled, holding back tears. She offered a bleary smile. "Oh, you are too good to me!"

Susannah waved it off. "Nonsense. I've had Christina cooped up in my home for too long. But as luck would have it, she is a marvelous cook. It sounds like you could do with an extra pair of hands. We can spend the day with you today, and we can come again if you would like."

"Yes!" Eleanor nodded furiously, pulling them inside. She brushed a hand across her cheeks, spreading flour over them. "If you don't mind, yes. I'll be happy to pay you!"

The surprise was visible across Christina's face and Susannah grinned. "All I need is the chance to spend some time with little Susie. But I do believe Christina could do with some extra purse money. Why don't you show her your kitchen?"

"Right, right." The woman was scatterbrained as she led them through the house.

Susannah stayed with the women for a few minutes until Christina relaxed, and then went to see to the fussy child. Throughout the afternoon, she returned often to the kitchen to check on the women and see how they were doing. Lucas was right as usual for every time she looked in, her friends looked happier and brighter.

Chapter Eleven

Christina

"Just like that, only a little harder. Right, put your elbow into it. Nice and firm, very firm." Eleanor watched Christina's hands closely, nodding. The scrutiny was similar to what she had felt back in Virginia, by everyone in town who stared her down.

But this was different, for the other woman didn't appear to care about what she looked like at all. She only seemed to want the pie crust to be perfect. It was a refreshing sensation, and she could feel herself working harder to make sure she did her best. When the woman fell silent, Christina glanced up from the table to find Eleanor nodding with a relieved smile.

"Is this good?" Christina raised an eyebrow as she waited to hear what Eleanor had to say.

Eleanor grinned. "It's perfect. You're such a quick learner. I cannot thank you enough. These are the last ones we'll do for the day. I'm tired and you must be, too," she added after a moment, working on her own crust.

The two of them worked quietly for a few minutes until they heard humming, and Susannah arrived with a young girl in her arms. The child was nestled into the crook of her neck as she walked carefully down the hall, humming and rubbing a hand across the back soothingly. It was a natural look for a woman and child, making Christina curious why Susannah didn't have any children of her own.

"How is she?" Eleanor asked in a whisper, handing the berries over to Christina.

"Sleeping," Susannah murmured, swaying as she slowed down. "Susie's going to be just fine. And her little brother is resting as well," she added after a moment. "I wanted to come and see how you two were getting on."

The women glanced at each other as Eleanor nodded. "We're just about done for the day." Eleanor looked at Christina and smiled. "She's everything I needed, Susannah. I've never known a more efficient cook, Christina, and that's saying something."

"It is," Susannah agreed with a nod, before she started humming again. "I'll be back after I put her down," she sung softly on her way out.

Christina watched her go and then sneaked a glance towards Eleanor as well. They were such lovely women, inside and out. How was that possible? They treated her with a respect that she'd never known from anyone outside her family. Was this what it was like to be a normal person?

She had to wonder then, if the rest of the town could be nice as them. But that felt like too much to hope for. Biting her lip, she shook her head to prevent dreams like that from taking root and tried to focus on putting the finishing touches on the pie. Once the top crust was there, she sprinkled sugar on top and pushed it further onto the table.

Eleanor had completed her pie as well and grabbed them both to put in the oven. "I can't believe it," she announced when that was completed. "We're done! It's done. Ten pies all in one day. Why, I've only ever been able to do four." Coming over, she grabbed Christina's arm. "Please, please tell me you'll come again. I'm begging you."

She looked at her with such earnest sincerity, Christina couldn't help but nod. "Of course. That is, if Mrs. Jessup is all right with that."

As they continued discussing her coming again, Susannah arrived and they took care of the details. The Jessups rarely needed both their horses in one day so Christina would take one of their horses and a cart over to the Connor's ranch three days a week and help with the pies. Orders would slow down soon with summertime, or so Eleanor hoped. This would give her the aid she needed, and it would also have Christina doing more than just helping at the boarding house. On top of this Eleanor still promised her payment for her services, and Christina rode home still trying to imagine that. Money just for herself. This was new and exciting.

What would she even do with it? The expenses she had to pay for her rent at the boarding house came from her mother's savings and some from her aunt and uncle. That money had a purpose and she didn't feel she had the freedom to use it for anything but room and board since she didn't know how long she'd be with the Jessups. Though in her childhood her mother had attempted to give her a few coins for candies in the past, there were always other children around to relieve her of them. What would she do with extra money now?

It occupied her thoughts into the next afternoon when she returned to the ranch. The Jessups' horse, Lemondrop, knew the path well and guided her right to the barn. Men were already there working with a few of the horses and helped her off the cart just like they had the previous day. Christina thanked them and hurried up to the kitchen where Eleanor Connor welcomed her with a smile.

She was a lovely woman, tall with dark hair, and still an Eastern accent. Her children were precious, the little ones who slept or played noisily nearby. Little Susie was getting over her cold very well and insisted on racing around the house, bringing toys to her baby brother and making him coo. It warmed the house with an energy Christina had never experienced, and she was a little disappointed when they finished their work for the day.

"Thank you again so much, my dear." Eleanor hugged her tightly and then handed over a few coins, enclosing them carefully into Christina's hands. "I'll see you on Friday?"

Nodding, she stepped back and squeezed on the coins. "Yes, Friday. You're very welcome. Have a lovely evening," Christina added, and turned down the steps of the house. Her boots hit the ground and she took a deep breath. And back to the boarding house she was ready to go.

The young woman fiddled with the coins as she went. Eleanor had wanted to pay her more, but it was all Christina was willing to take for now. And even still, it was plenty of payment. If she ever went into town, she pondered, would she finally be able to purchase a piece of hard candy?

Her eyes wandered as she walked towards the barn. Shivering at a gust of wind, Christina paused and squinted. There was someone on the other side of the fence who caught her eye. A set of broad shoulders was brushing a beautiful dark brown horse. It was a beautiful scene against the mountains and she was drawn in that direction. When she reached the post, she realized her assumptions were right.

It was him. Mitchell Powell. Of course she was drawn to him. He was handsome and she liked him.

The man was near the fence tending to the horse in the pasture. A soft wind brought his soothing voice in her direction though she couldn't hear the exact words. Leaning against the fence, she watched him for a moment before gathering the courage to speak up. "Good afternoon," she called out as she waved to him.

Turning around to her, Mr. Powell stared for a minute before tipping his hat. He glanced around before he beckoned, inviting her into the pasture. Christina hesitated only a moment before ducking her head and climbing between the wooden fence posts. Since they had last seen each other a week or so ago, the man had confused her. Their light conversation had been fun, or so she had thought, until he had left so suddenly. She had half a mind of asking him about it outright but was hesitant now to address it.

"Miss Bristol." He tipped his hat to her.

It reminded her then of the spot she had seen on his cheek before, probably a birthmark. When they'd met, Mitchell had been confident enough to take off the hat, but it was different today. His hat remained firmly on his head. But she didn't care at all since she could hardly notice anything else after looking into his bright cornflower blue eyes. "Mr. Powell." She didn't even bother to try to hold back her smile.

"How are you this afternoon?" He turned his head slightly so she could only see the side of his face that didn't have the birthmark.

She knew what it was like to suffer stares and judgement from others so she didn't judge him for this insecurity. How could she?

Slipping the coins inside her coat pocket, she wrapped her arms around her middle. Christina smiled hopefully. "Chilly now, but good. I'm doing very well. And how are you, Mr. Powell?"

He nodded. "Good, thank you."

Silence ensued, and she considered leaving if he wasn't going to say anything. He fidgeted, and her eyes turned to the horse. "Is he yours?" Christina asked hesitantly. "He's lovely."

Turning away, she noticed how he pulled the collar up to hide his face again. Maybe it was her that he was uncomfortable about, Christina realized. She swallowed. "Actually, it's a her. And yes, she is lovely. Mr. Connor has brought in a herd that needs breaking in, and I have experience in taming Mustangs."

"That's amazing," she offered hopefully, and paused. "Can Mustangs be girls? I always thought…"

He shrugged when she trailed off, fiddling with the rope harness in his hands. "Mustangs are wild horses. They gather like a family, with a mare and a stallion to lead them. A mare is female, and a stallion is male. This one is going to belong to Mrs. Connor." Mitchell smiled and his eyes lit up. This time, she also noticed the sharp jaw line angled towards her. Oh yes. He was a very handsome man, indeed, and she really wanted him to look at her.

"She's a fortunate woman," Christina breathed softly as she looked at the animal. It was around his height, a deep brown that might even match Mrs. Connor's hair, with a white star on the forehead. Cocking her head, she sighed. "Oh, she is lovely."

Mitchell's gaze was still on her. "Would you…um, do you want to brush her?"

Surprised, she looked to see if he was teasing her. But he almost looked happy and she bit her lip. Maybe he wasn't annoyed with her after all. It was difficult to tell what he was thinking. "What? Oh, could I? Although I'm afraid I don't know how to pet a horse." Christina cleared her throat anxiously. "Brush her, I mean. Not pet her. Horses aren't petted, are they?" She bit her lip to make herself stop talking. What had come over her?

He chuckled and stepped back. "It's easy. She's very calm, and I have her in case anything happens." He showed her the rope. "Horses use their nose as their primary sense. You'll want to approach her from the front, never from behind, and put out your hand. Move slowly and let her sense you."

Respectfully, she obeyed and walked through his instructions to the best of her abilities. Christina stepped closer and closer and felt the animal huff, spreading warm air across her hand. She'd taken off her gloves and though her fingers felt frozen, she was thrilled at the chance to touch this horse. Back home on the farm, they had two horses but she had never touched them. Her uncle loved them so much, that no one else ever tended to them. But there had always been a part of her hoping to someday brush them, or even ride one.

Her breath caught when she was given the opportunity to touch her gorgeous mane. Christina stopped, surprised at the thickness of the creature's hair. In awe, she stopped and looked at Mitchell. "She really is lovely," she whispered.

Mitchell nodded, fixing his hat. After a minute of angling with the rope harness, he switched sides to stand beside her. One hand on the rope, the other brushed the horse with her. "She is. Probably the prettiest of the bunch, but don't tell her mother." The joke surprised Christina and she laughed in delight. "But you're right, she is lovely. They all are. Horses are incredible animals, and I've always loved working with them. There's nothing I'd rather do."

The passion seemed to exude right from him and tingled in the air. Christina looked up at him thoughtfully and smiled at the look in his eyes as he brushed the Mustang. It gave her the courage she needed to take a deep breath and ask, "Mr. Powell, would you be willing to teach me to ride a horse?"

Chapter Twelve

Susannah

Rain was steadily falling on the other side of the window. This weather wasn't what Susannah wanted. Humming anxiously, she squinted harder and kept her eyes out for the trail. Any minute they should be coming, she told herself, any minute now.

"Aha!" she cried out triumphantly, slapping the chair she was kneeling on. "They're coming, Lucas, they're coming!"

He mumbled something from the hallway but she didn't bother looking behind her. Now that she had them in her sights, Susannah didn't want to let them go. Eagerly she kept looking out, squinting as the tiny moving figures slowly became bigger and more life sized.

It was early spring, and a few weeks had passed since the young Christina Bristol had begun going to the Connor's ranch to help with the piemaking process. Things were going well, but she had noticed the other week that someone was riding home with her.

Eleanor had mentioned it but hadn't been able to

say much at the time. It had been after church and the children were making a fuss. Susannah shifted in her spot, biting her lip. Clearly the two of them had grown close enough that he had escorted her home like this more than once. How long had this been going on? She could only wonder.

Not only was this thrilling, it was equally relieving. Susannah had been pouring over possible suitors for a while but none of the possibilities seemed right. Perhaps he would, whoever it was. What if he was a suitable match all on his own? Susannah watched them carefully, following them as they went around the house and towards the barn. Once they were closer, she ran to the back door. Pulling on her cloak, she was already wearing her boots and snatched a scarf on her way outside. She had to meet him this time.

He was helping her off the cart as Susannah reached them. Her chest heaved in the rush and her breath was visible before her in the cold air. She shined as she saw their hands linger together. "Hello, you two," she offered brightly.

Christina looked up in surprise. The man turned, and that's when Susannah realized she did know him. It was the man that had visited with Matthew Connor. What was his name again? "Howdy." He dipped his hat her way politely. "Good to see you again, Mrs. Jessup. Ma'am."

Beaming, Susannah glanced between them. They stood close to each other, and she could hardly suppress the excitement bubbling inside her. "It's wonderful to see you again as well," she assured him. "I wanted to invite you for supper. That is, we'd love to have the Connors and yourself over to supper. It's been too long. Do you think Thursday might be too soon?"

After glancing down at the ground, the man shrugged. "Uh, no. No, I think that should be all right. That's mighty nice of you."

Susannah chuckled and shook her head. "Nonsense. We would love to have you. If you bring her home again tomorrow, perhaps you can let me know if Thursday is a good day?"

The two of them glanced at each other and she tried to understand their gazes. There was clearly something between them, but she couldn't be certain about what it was exactly. Had they spoken of a courtship? Were either of them pursuing it? Oh, she certainly hoped so. The two of them were just darling together.

"All right." Mitchell nodded finally. "I'll do that." Then he glanced at Christina and tipped his hat to her. It gave Susannah a chance to notice that while he avoided giving her a straight look, he didn't shy from Christina's gaze.

So she took a step back, gradually realizing she was in the way. "Lovely. Well, I'll be going, then. Thank you, good sir." Trying not to smile too much, Susannah hastened back to the house. Still wrapped up, she turned around as soon as she got in the door to watch the couple. Just because they didn't want her there didn't mean she couldn't stop for a look, right? She bit her lip and watched them curiously.

Most would turn towards putting away the horse and cart. Young people falling in love would draw closer and closer, talking more and more quietly. Christina and Mitchell chose another course by unhitching Lemondrop to put away the cart, and then fixed the harness on the horse. What were they doing? Susannah squinted.

That's when something touched her hip and she shrieked in surprise. Clasping a hand over her mouth, Susannah whirled around to find Lucas's merry gaze looking down on her. Eyes wide, she smacked his chest. "I can't believe you!" She hissed, trying to keep her voice down. "What if they had heard me scream?" Hurriedly she peeked out the window again and sighed in relief when they never looked at the house. "You're terrible," she mumbled "They could have heard you."

His hand cupped her shoulder, but she was prepared this time and didn't scream. "That was you, dear. I didn't scream." He chuckled and carefully unwound the scarf from her shoulders. "What are you snooping on this time?"

She hummed a few notes in delight. "Lucas! Will you look at this? Come see. Mitchell has taught Christina how to ride."

"Ride what?"

Reaching back blindly, she slapped his leg. Lucas just took the opportunity to unbutton her jacket and slip it off her shoulders. "Ride a horse, of course. What else would she ride, silly?" Susannah beamed as she moved some of the curtain aside to see better.

They watched as Mitchell patiently helped her onto the horse where she started out sitting side saddle, but after making two circles around him, she moved one leg to the other side. Susannah reached out and found Lucas's hand, squeezing it tightly. Lucas fidgeted but took a seat beside her, running his other hand through her hair.

Horses made her nervous, so she tried not to be

around them too often. It was Lucas's job to tend to their horses and to teach the young women to ride. Susannah had been putting that off for Christina, she grudgingly acknowledged, but wondered if that decision hadn't turned out to be a blessing in disguise.

Mitchell's hands waved in the air slowly as he spoke to her. Christina was stiff, but she kept her eyes on him as she did what he told her to do. Susannah saw that much. At one point the young woman slowed down, but as Mitchell started over, Lemondrop moved away teasingly and the girl's head was thrown back in laughter. Susannah squealed. "Oh, they are precious! Are you watching? Lucas?"

"Well, I can see they're having fun together, that's clear. But don't you think maybe we should give them some privacy? And I'm getting hungry. Could we get started on that?" He stepped back and put his hands on his hips as he pursed his lips.

Soon, Christina stepped breathlessly inside and joined them in the kitchen. She didn't say a word about what she'd been doing, and only spoke after Lucas inquired about her day. Susannah wanted to ask her all about Mitchell but managed to restrain herself.

The following days were just as difficult as she was forced to conceal her enthusiasm while preparing for their guests. Susannah invited the young woman to cook for the occasion, knowing how much she loved working in the kitchen and also knowing it would impress the young Mr. Powell when he found out that she'd prepared most of the supper meal.

When Thursday evening finally arrived, Susannah was folding the last napkin when they heard the cart pull up just outside. She jumped excitedly and turned to

Christina with a nod. The young woman hastily fixed her hair before pulling off her apron and heading towards the door. She wanted to follow but Lucas stepped over and rested a heavy hand on her shoulder.

"Right." She nodded hurriedly at his unsaid words and gave him a smile. He didn't need to say anything to get his point across, to make sure she was attentive and not overbearing. *Don't say anything,* she told herself, *just wait and see how it goes. Just listen.* The front door opened and a squeal escaped her lips before she clapped a hand over her mouth. "Sorry."

Lucas just chuckled and kissed her forehead before placing his hand on her back to guide her to the hall towards their guests. His long gait slowed to match hers and Susannah eagerly went to greet their friends, wrapping her arms around Eleanor and then Matthew. She shook hands with Mitchell afterwards, beaming cheerfully to everyone.

Clasping her hands together, Susannah glanced at them all. "Welcome, all of you! Come in, come in. Take your coats off, please. Let's all get comfortable, shall we? Supper is waiting on the table. Christina cooked the meal, and it smells wonderful. Don't you think?"

Everyone nodded eagerly and they went to the table to be seated, and Susannah sat across from Christina and Mitchell. Grinning around the table, she nodded and motioned to the young man. "Mr. Powell, would you do us the honor of offering grace?"

He hesitated before finally nodding. Then he pulled his hands together and clasped them on top of the table. Everyone copied his action and bowed their heads.

"Dear Father, we thank You for the gift of fellowship with each other as Your children. We appreciate the way You care for us with rain and sunshine, alike. But now, bless this meal. Bless the Jessup family for their kindness. And bless Miss Christina for preparing this lovely supper. Amen."

It was a delicious meal of tender roasted chicken with green beans and glazed root vegetables. There was fresh bread as well, and a Dutch apple pie for dessert.

"Oh, this was wonderful. What a lovely meal!" Eleanor put a hand over her belly and sighed once she was finished eating. "I do enjoy eating food that I haven't had to make, I will say that." They laughed and she shook her head. "Christina, you work miracles."

The young woman blushed, looking down. "You're too kind."

Susannah grinned. "And you're too modest, my dear." She took another bite and glanced at Mitchell who had hardly said a word since saying the blessing. "Mr. Powell, what do you think of the food? You're rather quiet this evening."

"Perhaps I made the food too bland. Or possibly you're taken by surprise that I can actually cook?" Christina teased quietly, glancing at him. Then she blushed and looked back at her plate.

It was just a glance, but it was enough to show their comfort level with each other. Susannah nudged her husband who nudged her right back. Mitchell grinned at Christina. "Maybe if I can have a second helping, I can be a better judge."

Something was definitely there. Susannah wanted to reach forward and envelop the young couple in a tight hug before forcing them to hold hands. But she knew this wouldn't help. It made supper agonizing, waiting for them to look at one another. At one point, as Christina passed around the pie, she noticed their hands touch.

"Did you see them linger?" Susannah brushed her hair late that evening as Lucas readied himself for bed. She glanced over at him as his shirt came off, revealing a myriad of old scars and a few fading bruises. "Their hands?"

"No," Lucas snorted. "You're the one who notices that sort of thing. But there is something between them, I'll give you that."

"I knew you'd see it, too!" she cried out triumphantly, clapping her hands with glee. He just laughed and took the brush from her before taking over brushing her hair. Sighing, Susannah thought back to the young adults. They looked so young with their lives fully ahead of them. "I'm going to be good," she promised her husband quietly. "I'm not going to interfere this time, not one bit. Nothing more. I've done what I can, and I won't tell them to do anything, or try any tricks. They don't need me to figure this out. I realize that."

Her husband paused. "No interfering, really?"

Looking over her shoulder at him, she winked. "Sometimes it works without a push."

Chapter Thirteen

Mitchell

Mitchell glanced around the green pasture. It was a warm afternoon and a slight breeze picked up as he leaned against the fence. The sight before him was a lovely one and he suddenly realized he was smiling. He was happy, happier than he had been in a long time.

The sun was preparing to set. There was only a little bit of time left, but he would cherish every moment he had in the day. Looking back at the sight, he looked at the shoulders and the long dark hair. And the smile.

And he'd hardly noticed the horse.

This realization surprised him and he stepped back for a moment, hesitating as he tried to understand the sensation. Mitchell's heart was thudding and it wasn't from worry or tension. Gripping the fence post, he turned back to have another look.

Christina Bristol was a remarkably beautiful woman, inside and out. She was clever, passionate, and kind. Her life had been rough, from what she had told him so far, about her mother and growing up part Sioux. She even trusted him with her other name, Mahpiya. Life was good here and her happiness made his heart sing. And she never shunned him. Suddenly he appreciated the pounding heart even more for telling him the truth.

He grinned as she finished a loop around the pasture and turned his way. The moment she set eyes on him, Mitchell felt it. He fixed his jacket as she cantered the horse over cheerfully.

"Did you see that? Did you see me?" Her cheeks were flushed as she handed over the reins. She climbed down confidently and landed with both feet on the ground before turning to him again with that broad smile. "I can see now why you love horses so much. Oh, she's marvelous, isn't she?"

It took him a minute to find his voice. "Yes, she is," he mumbled, and glanced down at the reins. Taking a deep breath, he tried to think of something else to say but his feelings kept rising from his chest paralyzing his voice. Mitchell had to swallow them down before opening his mouth again. "Are you finished riding? Or did you want to do another lap?"

She hesitated and stroked the mare's neck and mane for a moment. "It's not too late is it?" She bit her lip as she looked at him with her deep dark chocolate eyes. "Just one more, perhaps, past the house? And you should join me! We never ride together," she added hopefully. "You'll join me, won't you?"

"Certainly," he told her immediately. "I'll get Rascal."

She waited patiently and Mitchell moved quickly though he tried to appear unhurried as he went for his horse. They rode together for a good hour before it was time for her leave, and they parted ways.

She took the cart home and he watched her go. Christina's fading figure grew smaller and smaller until she disappeared. Since he was supposed to be cleaning up that evening, he didn't have the time to escort her home. But Mitchell lingered, worried that the sensation in his chest would go away when she did.

The feelings didn't die even though she was gone. As he turned to tend to the horses and the barn for his evening duties, the warmth lingered in his heart. Over the next couple of days Mitchell couldn't stop thinking about her. What's more, he wanted her around. That's when it came to him, the idea to propose. If he could just muster up the courage, if she felt anything for him like he did for her, then it could be like this always. That thought made him smile.

"And come back before dark," Matthew added as he handed over a few more coins. "The boys said there have been bears out waking up hungry from hibernation and I don't want them getting any ideas about here. Be careful, yes?"

Mitchell nodded. "Of course, sir. I'll be back with everything before the sun sets." He tipped his hat and climbed onto his horse.

The ride was nice, and he liked the time he had to himself. There was a small part that he missed of the wild and not seeing folks for days, but Mitchell felt that those days were long behind him. It's not what he wanted anymore. Instead, he wanted this. Rocky Ridge, a home, and her.

He reached town and was finishing up the last of his errands by picking up some extra lace that Eleanor Connor had ordered. It was at the mercantile and he was waiting for the woman to bring out the material from the back when something sparkled and caught his eye. There was a small selection of jewelry at the front table, some simple and some elegant. It brought to mind a memory of his mother, who had looked at a lovely ring once with a sad look on her face.

"Didn't you have a ring?" he had asked her then, referring to the father who had passed away before he was born.

"I did," she had told him quietly before turning away. "A long time ago, before we had to sell it. But don't worry dear, jewelry isn't the important thing. The love is. Never forget it's all about love, not things."

She had loved her husband, Mitchell's father. As a young boy, he didn't understand what she meant, and had always hoped that he could give her the pretty things of the world like she deserved. But she hadn't lived long enough for that. Looking at them now, his heart pounded and he touched one carefully.

"What if Miss Bristol said yes?" His ears pricked at the mention of Christina's name, and heard tittering from around the room.

Mitchell froze. Slowing his breath, the man caught sight of two younger girls nearby playing with the basket of buttons. He was used to feeling eyes on him, but then he didn't expect them to be talking about him.

"You saw them at church," one murmured, her whisper carrying across the room. "Ma can't believe it. How could anyone be associated with someone who is disfigured that way?"

"Did you hear what Josiah said? Said he killed a man and that's how he got that thing on his face. Do you think the devil did that?"

"I should hope not."

"Here we are!" the woman sang as she came back to the counter. Mitchell jumped, and hastily he pulled up his collar and kept his eyes down as he paid, his thoughts running wild as he grabbed the fabric and hurried out. He didn't want to hear anything else those girls were gossiping about. He couldn't stand it that they thought he was ugly.

As he tried to pack everything into his saddle bags, he could feel the stares. Every time he cheated a glance beneath his hat, there were folks looking and Mitchell could just guess what they were saying about him. About his ugliness, his unnaturalness, that he was dangerous and possibly mean as the devil. Oh, it would be exactly what everyone else had ever said either to his face or behind his back.

"Let's get out of here," he muttered to Rascal as he swung into the saddle. What had he been thinking?

They were right. Even a fool could look at Christina Bristol and back at him only to immediately notice they didn't fit together. He was dumber than anything for having thought she might agree to marry him. How could he have ever thought that any woman, especially one as beautiful and brilliant as Christina Bristol, would ever want to be with him?

In disbelief, he laughed. And there he was, thinking about proposing to her. Mitchell shook his head. No, that wouldn't do. That would be too embarrassing for all of them. Swallowing the lump in his throat, he told himself to stop being foolish.

He could see clearly now.

When Sunday came around, he wanted to attend church and debated several times before deciding he had to deal with it at some point or another. After putting on his best jacket, Mitchell headed into town. After putting the horse into the stables, he started for his usual seat.

Except his regular seat was with her. Mitchell had been sitting with the Jessups and Christina for over a month now. He froze immediately, seeing her sitting reverently with her beautiful dark hair pulled into a loose bun. That old feeling was creeping back into his chest again. But this time, it hurt. Immediately he turned around and found an empty space in the back. He had deceived himself that they could remain as friends, but clearly that would be too difficult for him.

It wasn't as though she would miss him, Mitchell reflected. She probably wouldn't even notice that he'd stopped talking to her. She deserved better than him. Swallowing hard, he lowered the brim of his hat when he noticed Christina had turned to look around. She wouldn't be searching for him, he told himself, and didn't move.

When the sermon ended, he was one of the first ones outside. There would be no more lingering outside with Christina or anyone else. Mitchell retrieved Rascal and headed out of the stable.

"There you are!" Christina was right there as though she had been waiting for him. She squinted up at him, fixing her bonnet. "Why didn't you sit with us, Mitchell? I saved you your spot as always."

He glanced around hesitantly but paused when he saw several people staring at them. That was enough to support what he'd always known and Mitchell gritted his teeth. "I'm afraid I decided I won't be sitting there anymore," he said finally. "I prefer the benches in the back. Thank you, but it won't be necessary to save the space for me again. Have a good day, Miss Bristol."

As he left, Mitchell's heart thudded the entire ride home, breathless as he tried to confirm again this was the right thing to do. Best for Christina to not be put in a difficult situation. Best for Christina that she wouldn't be the center of gossip in town.

Chapter Fourteen

Christina

"But I was going to invite you over for cake," she murmured, watching Mitchell race away and completely dismayed he didn't wait for her to say a word. Christina squinted to be certain that his horse's tail hadn't suddenly caught fire, considering the way he raced away from her. What had happened? She'd seen him in the back sitting by himself and wondered why he hadn't joined her as he had in the past.

What had she done wrong? Swallowing, she straightened her skirts and tried to tell herself she was imagining things. Maybe he was busy. But then why did he say he wouldn't be sitting with her again? She was more than confused.

He didn't make any sense, saying he preferred the back of the church. They had discussed just the other week how those seats were newer but less comfortable. They agreed that sitting close to the front was much better than being in the back. Why was he lying now? Or had he been lying before?

If he honestly didn't want to sit with her when had he changed his mind? She had too many questions and no answers. Christina turned to the church house and then stared at the ground. She just wanted to be alone.

She tried to tell herself she was being unreasonable or that she had misunderstood. With a shake of her head, Christina took a deep breath and marched back over to Susannah and Lucas. They were a popular couple in town and always had people to talk to after the sermon. They didn't attend every Sunday since Mr. Jessup had to be on duty in the sheriff's office sometimes. She thought a break from having to speak to almost everyone in attendance was probably a good thing since it looked tiring.

Mrs. Jessup yawned as she finally returned to Christina and offered a smile. "Is he coming, then?"

Inhaling, Christina shook her head and tried to think. "No, I'm afraid he…um, I think he's busy," she managed. "On the ranch, there was something going on and he needed to help."

Susannah cocked her head over at her husband. "Really? We were just speaking with Matthew and he didn't mention a thing. I mean, I guess maybe he didn't think to tell us about an issue, but are you certain? Since when does that young man refuse your cooking?"

Usually she would have blushed at that remark but now it just pained her. Christina tried to chuckle about it, but the enthusiasm was dampened by her confusion. "Perhaps another time," she mumbled, and prayed they would leave soon. She could feel eyes on her, judging and laughing, and wanted to be away from it all immediately. Her head was in such a swirl when she just wanted to be alone and think.

"Of course," Susannah responded finally. Within a few minutes, they were able to gain Lucas's attention and detach themselves from the crowd. After Susannah gave one final hug to Rowena Jensen, the party of three returned to the Jessups' home.

The following Monday she returned to the Connors to assist in the kitchen with Eleanor. After getting a good night's rest, Christina had convinced herself she was only being silly and that everything would be fine once they saw each other again. It was a nice day so she rode Lemondrop instead of taking the cart and once she turned onto the ranch, she kept an eye out for Mitchell.

Lately, he was right outside the barn or in that small pen right where he would be able to meet her when she arrived. Mitchell was always there to help her unhook the cart and put away the horse. But that day he wasn't around. She paused Lemondrop in the doorway before entering the barn and looked about her hopefully.

Further towards the pasture and beyond the house, Christina was certain she recognized his hat. He was working with two horses and though he would have been sure to see her arrive, he'd made no move to join her. Though she lingered there for several minutes, Mitchell never came. Eventually, she had to put the horse away on her own and hurried to the house so she wasn't behind on the baking schedule.

Eleanor welcomed her inside and the two women hurriedly got to work. They were just taking a break to let the dough rest when there was a knock at the back door. Since Christina was washing her hands, Eleanor went to open it.

"Good afternoon, Mitchell. Please, come in." Christina froze the moment his name was mentioned.

"That's all right," he told Eleanor quietly. Christina had to scoot closer towards the hallway to hear. "I was just wondering if Matthew had left his brown belt behind? He's working on repairing a saddle and wants to use that until he can get that fixed. Thought it might work and wanted me to get that from you."

Eleanor laughed. "Of course. He's handy like that. I'll return in a moment." She left the door open and headed through the other room. As her footsteps faded away, Christina's heart pounded as she went to the open door.

He was right there, shuffling his feet and looking down. She was at the door by the time he looked up. Mitchell stepped back in surprise, but it wasn't the look that she had hoped for. Her smile slipped a little when he dropped his gaze again. Her stomach churned, and she started to believe that perhaps after all, she wasn't imagining things.

"I didn't see you this morning when I got here. I missed you," she said hesitantly, losing the confidence she'd had only a moment ago. Fiddling with the doorknob, Christina hoped he would just look at her. But his eyes moved everywhere else. "Is everything all right? How are you?"

Mitchell shrugged. "Busy."

She waited for something more, but that something more never came. "I see."

Dread filled her heart and she tried to think back. Had she done him wrong, or had something happened? Christina couldn't think of anything that had gone wrong. She had thought Mitchell was a good man, a gentleman she could trust. Usually he made her heart flutter and he could always make her smile but suddenly it felt as though everything was a lie.

Eleanor returned and they didn't have a chance to continue the conversation—one-sided as it was. Eleanor didn't notice the tension in the air, sending Mitchell on his way and joining Christina back in the kitchen. The young woman worked through the dough and accepted the harder job to crush the berries. It required a lot of muscle and energy, and there was enough on her mind that kept her moving.

She couldn't understand the abrupt change in Mitchell for it made no sense. It tormented Christina for the entire afternoon. Eleanor noticed she was quiet and invited her to help deliver the pies. After she accepted, the young ladies made their way into town and headed towards Dr. Fitzgerald's office.

"Mrs. Connor, is that you?" The cheerful man was already stepping out of his office and threw his hands up in the air enthusiastically. Eleanor's pace hastened so Christina did her best to keep up as they went to greet the man. She only knew of him from a distance, but her friend and employer welcomed him like an old friend. "Oh, it's good to see you, Missus! How are your children? Is Susie feeling better? My oh my, that must be my pie!"

Eleanor laughed and greeted him warmly. "It's good to see you, too! They are wonderful, just wonderful. I'm sorry it took me so long, but there've been quite a few orders. I don't know what it is, but everyone's been ordering these pies. If Miss Bristol hadn't come along to help me out, I don't know what I would have done."

The two of them started back towards his office and Christina slowly followed, not a part of the conversation and not wanting to intrude. She clutched the pie with both hands and watched her step. Eyes glued to the ground, the young woman listened to the sounds around her as she didn't want to trip and drop the pie.

Eleanor and the doctor were talking about her children, about Susie and her stomachaches. Then there were children out in the streets, playing sheriffs and outlaws and running all about. One of them burst out crying and she heard two others exclaim their apologies before helping with what sounded like a skinned knee. It made her smile. On the other street, there were women talking quietly, too hushed to be heard.

Behind her, there were stumbling steps. Two pairs, from the sound of it. Curiously, she slowed down and chanced a glance behind her. It was midafternoon, but it didn't appear to have stopped two men from drinking enough whiskey she could smell them even from that distance. Neither of them could walk straight and it mattered to them so little that the two of them had decided to bring their drinks with them out into the street.

What were they thinking? It was indecent, out in public like this where there were children and women. Christina thought about telling Lucas, since he was the town sheriff and on duty today, but she wouldn't know where to find him. But her heart beat quickly at the thought of addressing those two, an intimidating thought. She bit her bottom lip and decided that since they weren't being loud or hurting anyone, surely all would be well.

"Isn't that a pretty lady! She's got a nice bustle, ain't she? Why, I'd sure like a minute or two alone with her." His offensive words slurred into a blur from what she could hear. The man's drunkenness was suddenly loud, and Christina ducked her head, walking faster.

She looked ahead and heard the laughter behind her. Only a few yards off now, and Dr. Fitzgerald was opening his door for Eleanor. Christina swallowed, clenching the pie in her hands.

"What do you think you're doing, missy? We don't bite, ma'am." Muttering to one another, they were saying something she couldn't hear. On impulse, she glanced back, just out of curiosity. But somehow it was the wrong move. They stopped at the sight of her.

The man on the left laughed and nudged the other one with his elbow. "That ain't no woman! Look at that face. She's an Injun. Ted, you got yourself a squaw! Look at that!" He hooted, slapping his knee as he spilled his drink down the front of his shirt.

She hadn't heard words like those in months, but they still had the same effect as they always had before. Christina stopped in her tracks and she felt like the wind had been knocked right out of her. She clutched the pie, so hard the edge of the crust was crumbling. Deafened by the men's raucous laughter, she felt sick to her stomach and stumbled over to Eleanor.

She was still talking in the doorway to the doctor, laughing about something. When she reached them, they went inside and never even noticed what had happened to her. Christina shakily handed over the pie and took a seat on the bench as she stared at her boots. As her cheeks burned, she looked at her darker-skinned hands only to suddenly realize what it must have been.

So, that was why Mitchell had changed. Someone must have said something, and he had realized his error. Because she was a half-breed, it made her less of a human. Virginia had plenty of people who wanted to say that to her as well, so why wouldn't Colorado? There wasn't really any difference between there and here.

A tear escaped and splattered on her left boot. She hiccupped and hurriedly rubbed her cheeks, trying to hide anymore tears.

Glancing up, Christina was relieved to find that neither of them had noticed her dilemma. She felt lightheaded and suddenly wondered how they hadn't heard the two men. They had been loud enough. Or worse, had they heard and simply not cared? Her throat constricted. Perhaps that was it. They were only pretending, faking their kindness and warm feelings.

Christina had hoped that Rocky Ridge would be different. Her mother had hoped so as well. That was evident by the fact that she'd saved the advertisement for the Jessups.

But it was all the same. No matter where she went, people were the same. While there were a few folks who were good, like her aunt and uncle and the Jessups, most everyone had their reservations about her because of her heritage. Even Dr. Fitzgerald wasn't talking to her. And Mr. Powell? Why, Mitchell was probably playing with her, all the while planning to betray her like he'd just done.

In that moment, she came to the realization that she would never find true acceptance in Rocky Ridge. All of this was a mistake. The truth felt heavy on her shoulders as Eleanor finished her errands and they returned to the ranch. It was a quiet ride, and Christina was exhausted by the time they reached the house.

Bouncing her little boy on her hip, Eleanor frowned. "Are you certain you want to go so soon? I know it's a little late, but you're more than welcome to join us for supper. Perhaps you should stay the night. The sun is already setting and I'm not sure it's a good idea for you to try to go back alone."

"No!" Christina winced at how fast it came out. "I mean, I thank you. But I really do need to get back tonight." Pausing, she glanced down at the little girl hugging Eleanor's skirts. Susie glanced up and then hurriedly hid her face, trying to hide. There was a bitter taste in her mouth as she shook her head. "The Jessups will be expecting me. But, thank you again for your kind offer."

The ride home felt long and she invited Lemondrop into a gallop. All she could feel was the drumming of the hooves and she could only hear the wind brushed past her face. It helped her to think as she sorted things out. She would write a note to the Connors, to thank them for everything. And the Jessups she would need to say farewell to in person before finding a way to the train station. If she counted it right, there would be enough for a train ride and a little money left over.

Once Lemondrop was brushed down and she spoke to Mr. Jessup while he fed the cows, Christina sought out Susannah. The blonde was humming as she cleaned the fireplace but her smile faded as she turned around. "Oh dear. What's wrong, Christina? Are you all right?"

It had been easier to imagine and come up with words when it was just her and her head. But now that she was confronting Mrs. Jessup, she found herself hesitating. Clearing her throat, she shifted her feet and mustered up her strength. "I need to tell you that with a sad heart, I intend to return to my family in Virginia. I miss my aunt and my uncle, and desire to return on the first train ride back once I pack up."

"What?" Susannah's voice cracked and she covered her mouth before gathering herself again. "I thought you were happy. What about Eleanor? What about Mitchell?"

Swallowing hard, Christina dropped her gaze. "Mrs. Connor doesn't really need me anymore and Mitchell doesn't…he doesn't want anything further to do with me, I'm afraid." Susannah put out an arm to her but she moved back, pressed against the wall. "I'm very grateful for everything you've done for me. I've already spoken to Mr. Jessup and he said I can take Lemondrop into town and leave him with Mr. Jensen since I know there's one more evening train leaving tonight. I need to pack."

"I… I see…" Susannah managed faintly.

And Christina hurried out, unable to look at the woman who had been so kind again. She looked so lost with those big blue eyes and it was only hurting the two of them more. Off to her room she went, to pack her few belongings before leaving the boarding house for the last time. Her hands shook as she gathered her things, but she forced herself to keep moving. There were few places where she would be wanted, but she reasoned it was still better to be with those she was certain loved her.

Chapter Fifteen

Susannah

He repeated it again. "I assumed she had spoken with you. How was I to know?" Lucas ruffled his hair and took a deep breath. "But we can't tell her what to do, Susie darling. It's her life, her choice. If she wants to return home, then she has that right."

Shaking her head, Susannah paced the kitchen while rubbing her hands. Her mind was moving faster than a horse at full gallop as she sorted through the options. By the time the shock had worn off, Christina Bristol had already hugged her goodbye and left. Yet her heart was still racing and she couldn't stand still. "I know, I know. I just, I don't know what to do. You didn't see her face. You didn't see her anguish. I know she was heartbroken to leave."

"I talked to her, remember?" He pointed out patiently and offered a sympathetic smile. As she passed him again, he reached out and looped an arm around her waist to walk with her. "She made a decision to go and you must respect that."

She shook her head, thinking of the young woman. "No, I can't. There was something wrong. I could see it in her face. She was sad, Lucas, terribly distraught." Waving a finger in the air, she didn't let him make an excuse. "And it wasn't a normal sad, like when there are no more strawberries on the bushes. That's disappointing. But she was distraught, she was hurt, like something has happened. Something happened." Susannah stopped.

Beside her Lucas stopped as well, setting his other hand over hers. He had such a way of reaching her and helping her calm down, like a cool towel in the heat. As her husband had showed her several times, Susannah closed her eyes and took a long breath in before slowly releasing it. Something must have happened, she decided, something that had made her want to leave. Some other force had convinced her that she couldn't be there for some reason. But what could it be?

Why would she go back to Virginia? She was happy here, or at least, she had been. She couldn't have been acting a part all this time. Susannah could see it, the way she brightened up at church and loved going to the Connors' ranch. And the girl's face clearly displayed joy when she was riding Lemondrop. She'd taken to riding most evenings as though she were making up for lost time.

"I don't accept this," she said finally.

Lucas started to sigh. "Now, Susie, please…"

Shaking her head, she pulled her hand free of his. "No. Lucas, she talked little of her life in Virginia. All she said was that she needed a better life out here, meaning it had not been very good back there. The girl lost her mother and now wants to return after everything she has been doing here? I don't believe a word she said. Something else is going on."

"Fine," he said simply, and went to a window to look out. "The next train leaves in two hours, Susannah. She'll already be at the station by now. But from the sound of it, she didn't want to be bothered by anyone—not even you."

"I won't," Susannah said defensively, and brushed her hair back over her shoulders. "I'll just convince her." That was it, just what she needed to do. Nodding affirmatively, she straightened and went to the door. Then it hit her.

When Christina had been explaining why she was leaving, she had dropped her gaze when she said Mr. Powell's name. Her heart thudded. Whatever the concern was, it had to be about him. The gentleman hadn't been over since that Sunday he'd declined Christina's offer of cake. And it had just been the day before that Christina had confided in her, telling her how much she truly cared for Mitchell Powell. She was expecting an engagement, not this. How had this happened? Susannah had seen the way they looked at each other and there was no way things were just over this abruptly.

Lucas was saying something. She turned, opening her mouth sheepishly. "The cart," he repeated, and came over to give her hand a comforting squeeze. "Would you like me to put together the cart? I'm sure my horse would like an evening ride."

It hadn't come to mind that she would need to travel. Susannah was so focused on thinking it all through she didn't think about the effort and now her mouth went dry. "That will take too long," she groaned, and shook her head as she came to a resolve. "Coriander will do. Is he still saddled?"

"Yes, but I can do whatever you need me to do," Lucas offered as she started putting on her coat.

Shaking her head, she braced herself for it. "No, I can ride him myself."

"Susannah. I don't think that's a good idea."

But she didn't hear his protest. She was already out the door and down the stairs by the time his words were out.

The evening was growing late and there wouldn't be light out for more than an hour or two. Hopefully the sun wouldn't set before Susannah completed her mission. She was breathless as she went to the barn and found Coriander there. While Lucas wasn't a fan of naming the horses, Susannah found it helpful and thought it made them appear more friendly.

Her heart hammered. She'd ridden him a few times, but only once on her own and that was only because Lucas wanted them familiar enough with each other in case of an emergency. Well this was an emergency, she told herself, and untethered him from the post. "Hello, Coriander. Y-you like me, don't you?"

He shook his head, but she couldn't tell if it was more up and down or side to side. For a minute, she struggled with the saddle but he obeyed her. Coriander was much larger than Lemondrop, and even more uncomfortable for her. Susannah's breath was shaky as she tugged on his reins, wondering how anyone enjoyed being on these animals. Shutting down her fear as best she could, she reminded herself that horses were necessary, and they should be respected.

Finally, she got into position on Coriander and they

went on their way. Her hair blew past her in the wind and she squinted, trying to stay focused on the road. Focused on anything but the animal she rode. Coriander shook his mane again as she urged him even faster once they reached the main road. Eyes glued to the road ahead, Susannah gritted her teeth and tried not to think about the jarring run of the horse.

Lucas's horse was well-trained and fast, so she arrived quickly in the front yard of the Connor house. She moved to climb off and suddenly realized how far she was from the ground. It instantly made the world spin. Susannah gripped the pommel with wide eyes, hesitant to jump.

"Susannah?" Matthew stepped outside, putting his daughter down. "Whatever are you doing here? Did you need a cup of sugar?" he teased before hastening over. "Let me help you." He put a hand up to help her jump down.

Nodding, she swallowed and accepted it. "Yes, thank you. Not the sugar, no… Oh, here we go," she mumbled when she landed with two feet. Grabbing his arm, Susannah took a deep breath of fresh air. "I'm terribly sorry to inconvenience you, Matthew, but I need to find Mr. Powell. Is he around?"

"Mitch?" He shrugged. "I'm sure he is. The man hardly leaves the grounds. He's probably out in the pasture right now. Why? Is something wrong?"

She moved around Coriander to look over the pasture. There were several horses, and a few men nearby. But which one would he be? Frowning, she shook her head impatiently, but then realized that Matthew had asked her a question.

"No. Yes. I think so, I… I believe so, yes. Something

is wrong, but I don't know what it is. I just think Mr. Powell might have an interest in the happenings. Christina, um, Miss Bristol, is leaving," Susannah stumbled over her words as she followed him onto the porch to pick up Susie again. "Hey, sweetie." She managed a quick smile and a tickle under the little girl's chin. "I think something happened, and I thought Mitchell would know what it was. Unless you would? Or maybe she said something to Eleanor?"

Matthew's forehead creased but he only shrugged. "Here, hold Susie and I'll find Eleanor for you. We were just preparing supper." He handed over the girl and returned inside.

Little Susie's hair was growing darker like her parents' and was still curly. Susannah caught her breath as she bounced the little girl who was babbling innocently about her day. "Yes? And did you see Christina today, as well?"

"Tina?" Susie clapped her hands loudly. "Princess Tina!"

"Princess?" Susannah shifted the girl onto her other hip. She was growing up too fast, this precious little child. "Is Christina a princess?"

Nodding jerkily, Susie mumbled something and laughed. It made Susannah's heart ache at the sound, though there was so much joy in it. She was just letting the girl down to run inside as Eleanor arrived in her apron and covered in what looked like cranberry sauce.

"Susannah!" Eleanor gave her a hug without using her hands. "Whatever are you doing here? Matthew said that something happened to Christina?"

She swallowed and nodded. The moment sobered up as she glanced about and rubbed her chilled hands together. "She's leaving town, tonight. To return home to Virginia. She said she didn't want to stay. But I don't understand, and I think…well, did she say anything to you?"

The woman looked surprised as she shook her head. Eleanor wiped her hands on the apron as she leaned against the doorway. "No, she didn't say a word about going back, Susannah. Why, I was still expecting her to come tomorrow. I haven't paid her since last week. Oh my word. I didn't do anything to hurt her, did I? Matthew's never around so he never would and Susie's very quiet." Shaking her head again, Eleanor looked as worried as Susannah felt. "Why, I don't have a single idea what it could be. I don't know."

Susannah sighed and turned back to face the pasture. "I'm sure it wasn't you, dear, I'm sure it's fine. I'm going to make sure of that," Susannah added, and kissed her friend's cheek. "Thank you. Have a lovely evening!" And lifting her skirts the woman hastened down the steps, past Coriander, and into the pasture.

Once she was off the path, the ground grew uneven and she stumbled on her way to the fence. Without a second thought Susannah slipped between two posts though her dress snagged. It tore on the hem, but she paid it no mind as she started towards the first figure she saw, a man carrying a rope.

"Mr. Powell?" She called out. "Mr. Powell, sir?"

The man turned, and it wasn't him. He was thicker and shorter with a handlebar mustache. Susannah stopped as he eyed her warily. "Mitchell? He's over thataway. With the tan hat." He gestured vaguely. Susannah turned, squinting until she finally saw it.

"Mr. Powell!" She hollered, and waved a hand in

the air as she headed towards him. A few of the horses were near, but they stayed out of her path. Susannah was thankful for that, since she wasn't about to touch another horse, especially one she didn't know. A light brown one ran past her and she jumped, a hand over her heart.

Someone grabbed her when she stumbled. "Careful, ma'am."

To her great relief, it was him. "Mr. Powell," Susannah sighed in relief. "There you are. I need to speak with you. It's about Christina Bristol."

"Christina?" He fixed his hat, ducking his head. "Well, I, uh… I haven't seen her. We don't talk much, I'm afraid."

He was walking away before she could pull herself together. Susannah frowned in confusion, wondering what piece of the puzzle she was missing. The young girl had told her that he didn't want to have anything to do with her. She just had the nagging thought that something wasn't right here.

"Why not? That wasn't the case until quite recently," she demanded. Picking up her skirts, she made it through the grass and followed him. "What are you talking about? Miss Bristol is leaving town, and she's not coming back. It doesn't make sense. You need to go stop her, Mitchell. I know she'll listen to you. Please, you have to. She needs to stay here. She's been happy and she belongs here."

Looking up, she realized he was tending to a horse's hoof. Susannah stopped short and gripped her skirts hesitantly. Deep breath, she told herself. "Please, Mr. Powell," she repeated. "You need to stop her from leaving before it's too late."

Shaking his head, he concentrated on the horse. "I'm sorry, but I can't help you."

The horse huffed and Susannah jumped. "What? Why not?"

"She has the right to go if she wants," he muttered. "I can't make her do anything."

Susannah gaped at him in disbelief. Why were men like this? Why did they need to be so stubborn at the wrong time? "But…but she doesn't really want to go! She wants to be here. Christina loves this place, she loves Rocky Ridge. And most importantly, she loves you." The words came out more tentative than she had intended but they were true all the same.

He paused, and she grew hopeful. Susannah took a tentative step forward, but then he returned to his work. "Believe what you will," Mitchell told her gruffly, "but that's false. She wanted nothing to do with me."

"What?" Susannah slumped. "Why would you say that?"

Mitchell Powell gave it a final stroke on the neck before untethering the horse. Free, the horse glanced at them and broke away to go be somewhere else. "I'm saying that I couldn't do anything to stop her. She wouldn't— "

"Care?" She finished for him when he hesitated. Susannah crossed her arms and glared. He was taking too long and they didn't have time for this. A little voice told her now that nothing had happened. It was just that the two of them had let anxieties interfere without talking to each other. They'd made fearful decisions to avoid the possibility of getting hurt.

"Did she tell you that? I don't think she'd say that because it simply isn't true. Christina Bristol loves you,

Mitchell Powell. She told me herself that she had never met anyone more kind or more generous or more caring. I don't know what has gotten into you, young man, but that young lady wanted to marry you and the only thing standing in the way now is you. What on Earth is wrong with you?"

Chapter Sixteen

Mitchell

It was a shock he'd never experienced before.

It's not possible that she feels like I do, he told himself. But then he thought about it and realized something. She'd never turned away from him in disgust, and never shied from his touch. Mrs. Jessup was convinced Christina loved him and the woman wasn't a liar. Could she be correct? Christina Bristol was a beautiful woman, and she loved him. In that moment, that lighthearted feeling returned, where he felt like he was walking on air.

Until he grew nauseous. "Then I should go get her," he murmured, and she gave him a stern look. Immediately he ran towards the barn. "Thank you!" he shouted over his shoulder and never stopped.

"You're welcome!" she hollered, and there was a pause. "Send her back to our home, please!" He could have sworn she laughed. Mitchell leapt over the fence to the barn where he found his horse.

"Come here, Rascal." He opened the gate and swung

right onto him. He didn't need a saddle to ride and there wasn't any time to get it anyway. The animal still wore his rope harness and he clung to that and the mane as they tore through the yard. His hat flew off before he had a chance to pat it down, and he glanced back to see it float down.

But there wasn't time to stop and pick it up. Gritting his teeth, he shook his head. Mitchell took a deep breath and focused on the road. The night was growing late and the evening train would be there soon. If anyone had a chance of getting there on time, it was Rascal. Desperately Mitchell tried to understand what had happened, how he had let Christina slip through his fingers. He just hoped that the train hadn't arrived yet. And he hoped she'd hear what he had to say when he found her.

He was in luck. His horse was still slowing down when he jumped off and left him by the trough. Mitchell was breathless as he climbed the steps to the station, looking around wildly for that familiar head of beautiful rich, dark hair.

"Christina!" he shouted when he saw her and ran over breathlessly. The young woman had set her bag down and was watching the train tracks with her arms wrapped around her body for warmth.

She had heard and turned around. Confusion spread across her beautiful face. "Mitch—I mean, Mr. Powell. What are you doing here?"

"I had to come see you. I mean, stop you. Mrs. Jessup said that you were here, and I…"

The woman took a step back as she dropped her arms at her side and shook her head. "So? And what, you just decided that I can't leave? After you ignored me? After you shunned me?" A hurt expression crossed her face and settled on her pouty lips.

A moment of silence settled between them. He stared at her, wondering if he had heard her right. This wasn't the reaction that Susannah had hinted at. "But I only thought that you deserve—"

"Why would you do this?" Christina wouldn't let him finish and she leaned forward, splaying out her hands. "You can't just ignore someone and then come here when I'm leaving. I waited for you. After all our walks and our suppers, you just brushed me off, Mitchell. No explanations. No care for me at all. Who acts like that?"

He nodded, accepting that it had been his fault. He'd been a fool, and now it was time to fix that mistake. "I know, I know. I made a mistake, Christina. A big, foolish one. Please, I'm sorry. I shouldn't have treated you that way."

"You're right," Christina huffed, and angrily rubbed a hand across her cheek. "You shouldn't have. It was cruel and unnecessary. If you had a problem, any problem, you should have told me. If you didn't want to be around me, then you should have said something. But of all the ways you could have left me behind, your actions were deplorable. And hurtful beyond words. I have been trying so hard to change everything, and to be happy. I have been working and learning, and I thought we were, at least, friends."

He opened his mouth to try to respond, but she held up a hand to stop him. She shook her head and continued.

"Granted, I haven't had many friends in my life so I may be at fault here as well. I'm not completely aware of all the ways friends help each other. Do things usually go well and then suddenly go bad? Do people usually tell each other their secrets only to never speak again? Because if so, I guess I missed the whole purpose of friendship," she drawled angrily, throwing her hands up in the air. Mitchell stepped back hastily.

When she paused to draw in breath he thought she was slowing down. But he was wrong, and Christina spent another minute talking to him angrily. Though he attempted to apologize and clear up the mistake several times, she wasn't having it. People were watching them by that point and he couldn't decide whether he was angry also or just wanted to laugh. But another minute later, Mitchell had had enough.

The next time she put out her hands, he grabbed them and looked into her eyes, "I love you!" Mitchell caught her gaze as she froze. Her eyes widened into warm dark pools that felt like they were drawing in his very soul. It was a sensation he had nearly forgotten about and the feeling sent tingles through his body. From the top of his head to the tips of his toes, the young man was wrapped up in a feeling that made him feel invincible.

"What did you say?" Christina squeaked softly.

Grinning in relief, he tugged her to him. Mitchell felt the soft fingers entwined with his and his heart pounded. Christina was inches away now and all he wanted to do was wrap her in his arms.

"I want to talk now," he requested gently. "I have some important things to say." He spoke softly now, for he didn't want the rest of the world to know what was going on between them, especially since he was trying to figure that out as well. "Christina, I…of course I care for you, deeply. I've enjoyed every minute of your company and I look for you everywhere I go."

She gulped and took a shaky breath, her strength fading. Mitchell raised one hand and wiped away another tear that escaped down her cheek. "I wanted to ask for your hand," he admitted after a minute. "I had it all planned. But I stopped when I… I was certain you would reject me if I told you any of this. I hadn't asked to court you, and I was afraid I had been imagining what I hoped you felt for me."

She furrowed her brow and tilted her head to the side. She squeezed his hand but let him continue without being interrupted.

"After all, why would anyone accept me?" He offered a pained smile and looked into her eyes before he looked away. "I had my heart set on you even though I was sure it could only lead to pain. People can't look at me in the street, Christina, and I don't look at myself in mirrors. I can't help the way my face is, and I was afraid… Well, I was sure you'd feel…" Ashamed, he couldn't look her in the eye. "How could I ask someone as wonderful as you to marry a man like me?"

She slipped her hand away and brought it up to his imperfectly perfect cheek. Mitchell winced, expecting her to flinch. But she didn't pull away or frown or recoil. She cupped his face in her delicate hands. He had to close his eyes to gather his resolve and only opened them when he felt her lips on the cheek he hated so desperately.

Drawing away, Christina had a serious expression he couldn't read. She looked him in the eyes and finally smiled. "Mitchell, you are the most handsome man I've ever met. Most importantly, you're the kindest man I've ever had the pleasure of spending time with. Don't you dare doubt that for a moment. It's my decision about who I spend time with and who I don't."

Looking into the sincerity in her eyes, Mitchell felt a weight slip off his shoulders and his heart broke free. It was more than just her warm eyes that melted away the pain of the past. It was more than just her touch that made the lifetime of hurt and rejection fade away. It was her faith and her courage and her tenderness that made him whole in a way he had never been.

For the first time in his life, Mitchell was speechless. Taking a deep breath, he tried to think of something and found the only solution to thank Christina for this gift was to take her in his arms and kiss her. She wrapped her arms around him in response, smiling.

"Christina." And he grinned when she didn't respond, so he tried again. "Mahpiya?"

"Hmm?"

He smiled against her lips. "Will you marry me? Please say yes."

Her giggle tickled against his cheek. "It's about time you got around to that. Yes, I'm honored to marry you."

In just about an hour, everything changed for Mitchell. Though he'd been sadly resigned to the idea of a lonely life, that evening he escorted Christina back to the Jessups and returned to the Connors as a new man. A man with a life of love and an amazing woman who would soon be his wife.

He felt joy and hope he'd never known before. He believed in God, though his faith was quiet but steady. Praising Him as he settled in for the night, he said a brief prayer of thanksgiving because he had no doubt God had led Christina to him.

Chapter Seventeen

Christina

Christina and Mitchell shared their happy news with the Jessups and Connors the following day after all the confusion had been made right. Christina wrote to her aunt and uncle immediately to share the story of her upcoming nuptials and her newfound happiness. Not knowing if they'd be able to make the trip or not, she invited them anyway. She prayed they'd be able to make the journey and was delighted to get a quick response.

Aunt Ruby and Uncle Steven were thrilled with her news. And she was beside herself with joy that her only family in the world would be with her when she married Mitchell, her true love.

Now that they knew when her aunt and uncle would arrive, they set the date for the following month. Life turned into one happy blur. Mitchell worked harder than ever to save up for a small cottage for the two of them and Christina helped sell more pies so they could furnish their home.

Their wedding was on a beautiful, cloudless Wednesday morning, and Christina Bristol dressed in a pretty pale blue dress that she knew matched his eyes. Her aunt and uncle cried joyfully when they were pronounced husband and wife. Christina clung to him, happy and hopeful for their new life together.

She'd expected to get emotional and nostalgic when she became Mitchell's wife. She'd taken care to have a white lace handkerchief tucked into her sleeve just in case she needed it. The tears never came, though. While she wished her mother and father could be with them and meet the man she loved with all her heart, she knew that God's will was being done. All things happened in His own time and she accepted that.

After the ceremony, their family and friends were invited to the newlyweds' new home for supper. It was a bold undertaking for Christina to cook a meal on the same day she became Mitchell's bride, but she was overjoyed to do it. Cooking was one of her loves and she wanted to share something special with the people who'd helped her find her perfect match.

On the ride home, Mitchell drove with Christina snuggled next to him. She knew she'd never get tired of having his arms around her and feeling close to him. She felt safe and cherished and she never wanted this feeling to go away.

When they all pulled up outside the Powell cottage, everyone waited for the newlyweds to get down and lead their first guests into their home. Mitchell took Christina's hand and started to lead everyone into the house.

"Wait!" Matthew called before they got inside. "Not just yet!" When he hurried around the other side of the house, Mitchell and Christina glanced at each other in confusion and then to Eleanor. She was helping Susie off the cart and holding her other child on her hip.

"Don't look at me." She grinned. "I wanted to give you a quilt for your wedding present."

"Oh, but I—" Susannah started and fell quiet, glancing up at Lucas who shrugged impassively. An awkward silence surrounded them and Christina slipped her fingers through Mitchell's just as Matthew called for them.

Everyone turned to find Matthew leading out a small gray horse with one white stocking. Immediately Mitchell recognized it as one of the few horses left from the herd that hadn't been purchased. Most of the buyers were men on the trails and often overlooked the smaller ones though they were often faster. He looked at his boss's delighted expression and made the connection.

"Oh, she's lovely." Christina pulled him towards the animal, greeting it gently. "Mr. Connor, is this one yours? Though she's young, I think she'll be an excellent horse. But why is she here?"

Laughing, Matthew set the reins in her hands. "She's a wedding present! Your home has already been stocked with most of your needs, and I thought this might be the perfect gift. We all saw you learning to ride with Mitchell's help and we saw how much you loved it. Besides," he added most softly, "I don't think she could do any better than live with the two of you."

Everyone cheered as it dawned across Christina's delighted face. "Oh!" She hugged Matthew and then Mitchell before turning back to the horse. Mitchell watched with pride as she ran her hands across the beautiful creature before meeting his gaze again. The two of them loved horses, and it brought joy to his heart knowing she understood them like he did.

Holding the reins, she returned to Mitchell's side. "Thank you," they chorused to Matthew. "I'll put her away," Mitchell offered. "Why don't you take our guests into the house and start dishing up that special roast beef feast we've been hearing about, my love?"

With a wink, she nodded. Mitchell led both horses to the pen for their oats and water. Once they were settled, he returned and stepped into the house. He went right to Christina's side as if he couldn't stand being away from her for another moment.

Standing near Susannah and Lucas, Christina watched how they interacted. Clearly they were deeply in love. She looked up at Mitchell with a quirky smile as they overheard the conversation.

"I'm glad it worked out," Susannah was telling her husband as Eleanor was passing their baby boy over to Lucas. "I was required to stay out of the way for the most part, I know, but I believe I'm really getting good at this matchmaking."

Lucas chuckled and teasingly elbowed her. "You didn't do anything, dear. You can't take any credit for this one."

She scoffed. "Oh, you know I'm right. I'm quite good at matchmaking. Getting better all the time."

Christina giggled as she looked up at her new husband. There were a lot of windows that invited the sunshine into the room, with a large enough table that fit all their friends. Everyone was happy to be there in the place they now called their own.

"Of course you are, dear. Better all the time." Lucas grinned and looked away.

"Wait, are you mocking me? You'd best not be mocking me."

He was bouncing the little boy, and focused on the little one as he continued to grin. "Heavens, no, Susie. I'd never do that."

Taking the child, Susannah beamed at the boy before pouting at her husband. "You are mocking me. That's not very nice. If you keep mocking me, I won't kiss you anymore."

Mitchell moved around to one of the open seats and winked at Christina who paused beside the bickering couple. She hesitated, seeing the look of consternation on Lucas's face. Even Ruby and Steven, Christina's aunt and uncle, looked concerned. But Matthew and Eleanor were laughing. Indeed, a moment later, Lucas looked like he was about to apologize when his wife smirked and suddenly kissed him long enough that they both blushed bright red.

"You thought I was serious for a minute there, didn't you?" Susannah laughed out loud and gently bumped her shoulder against her husband's arm.

Lucas chuckled and shook his head. "Doesn't happen often, so I suppose I can give you this one, especially since there were witnesses."

The baby squealed as they separated, and the Connors laughed as they took the boy back. "You two are as troublesome as our children," Eleanor teased. "Besides, we should be cheering for the newlyweds, not you old folks."

Lucas and Susannah protested lightly, laughing as they settled back in their seats. The attention turned towards the Powells as Christina hugged her aunt and joined them at the table to eat the lovely meal she'd prepared to celebrate the happiest day of her life.

Epilogue

Though Christina always pulled her hair back and out of her face in a bun or into braids, the silky tresses usually escaped. The wisps would flow over her shoulders and down her back. Her almost black hair used to bother her, but Mitchell had assured her time and again that he loved her hair.

They'd been married for six blissful months. Christina grew happier every day. She'd never dreamed her life could be this good. She woke up every morning with a prayer of rejoicing for the miracles God was bringing forth in her life.

She was still self-conscious that her skin was a bit darker than everyone else's and she knew she still looked different than everyone she saw. That was an insecurity she was struggling to shed.

She also knew that Mitchell's appearance drew stares in town from people they didn't know. His birthmark didn't bother her in the least and it never had. In fact, she loved it because it was him.

Though they both loved the things about the other that made them unique, individually they were slowly realizing that it didn't matter what other people thought. They could easily face down the stares and much more when they were together.

And now as she prepared to share her special secret with her husband, she thought of her parents. How happy they'd be to see how things had turned out for her in Rocky Ridge! She'd been reluctant to come to an unknown place, but this was where she'd found her future. She had no regrets.

The slamming back door pulled her out of her musings and she smiled at the thought of seeing her husband. "Supper's almost ready, Mitchell. Hungry?" She turned and smiled as he came to her.

"Starved. But I can wait a minute if you'll give me a kiss."

"I think that's something I can manage." She giggled and stepped into his arms as she raised her face to his. Their lips met and she felt the familiar quiver she cherished.

He pulled her close and she heard him sigh.

"You know, Mitchell, I was going to save this for after supper, but maybe now's just the right time."

"What is it? Is anything wrong?" His brow furrowed as he leaned back to look at her.

"Oh, don't worry. Everything's fine. It couldn't be better, actually." She smiled and he looked puzzled. "Come with me and let's sit."

They sat on the settee in front of the fire and she reached for his hand. She thought he might have figured out her news but chuckled as she realized he was completely in the dark.

"All right, Christina. What's going on?" He tilted his head, still not smiling.

"Well, I saw Dr. Fitzgerald today—"

"Dr. Fitzgerald? Why didn't I know you were seeing him? What's wrong?" He looked like he was going to cry.

Feeling a little sorry for him, she decided to come out with the news rather than torture him further. "I'm with child, Mitchell. We're going to have a baby."

Relief and joy covered his face at once. "A baby? I can't believe it!"

"I know it's soon, but I'm happy. What do you think about it?"

"Well, it's unexpected news. I knew we'd have children, but I didn't think we'd have a family so soon. It's what I want and once I get used to the idea of being a father I'll be thrilled."

She smiled and reached for his hand, content to sit with him for a moment as they both let the news sink in.

"Christina, on the day we married I thought about this day. It's come sooner than I expected, but that doesn't matter. The thing I promised myself was that our children would have two names—just like their mother."

Her jaw dropped in surprise. She was speechless as she watched his face.

"I'm sorry I never met your parents, but I want us to pay tribute to them. We can give them Sioux names and Christian names. And I want to teach them about their heritage. Is that something you'd like to do?"

A tear slid down her cheek and she wiped it away slowly, unashamed and touched. "I'd love that. I love it more that you thought of it. It's the best gift you've ever given me. Thank you, Mitchell."

He put an arm around her and pulled her close again.

She melted into him as she thanked God again for his mercy and grace and for sending this perfectly imperfect man into her life. Together they could accomplish anything. She couldn't wait to meet their baby and start raising their family. Together.

* * * * *

WE HOPE YOU ENJOYED
THIS BOOK FROM

LOVE INSPIRED
INSPIRATIONAL ROMANCE

Uplifting stories of faith, forgiveness and hope.

Fall in love with stories where faith helps
guide you through life's challenges, and discover
the promise of a new beginning.

6 NEW BOOKS AVAILABLE EVERY MONTH!

"You don't ever complain. You take care of someone
else's *kinder* without hesitation, and you're giving them a
home they haven't had in who knows how long."

"Trust me. There was plenty of hesitation on my part."

"I do trust you."

Beth Ann's breath caught at the undercurrent of
emotion in his simple answer. "I'm glad to hear that. I got
a message from their social worker this afternoon. She
was supposed to come tomorrow, which is why I stayed
home today to make sure everything was as perfect as
possible before her visit."

"I wondered why you didn't come to the project house
today."

"That's why, but now her visit is going to be the day after tomorrow. What if she decides to take the children and place them in other homes? What if they can't be together?"

Robert paused and faced her. "Why are you looking for trouble? God brought you to the *kinder*. He knows what lies before them and before you. Trust *Him*."

"I try to." She gave him a wry grin. "It's just…just…"

"They've become important to you?"

She nodded, not trusting her voice to speak. The idea of the three youngsters being separated in the foster care system frightened her, because she wasn't sure what they might do to get back together.

"Don't forget," Robert murmured, "as important as they are to you, they're even more important to God." His smile returned. "How about getting some Christmas pie before we have to fish three *kinder* out of the brook?"

With a yelp, she rushed forward to keep Crystal from hoisting Tommy to see over the rail. Robert was right. She needed to enjoy the children while she could.

Love Harlequin romance?

DISCOVER.

Be the first to find out about promotions, news and exclusive content!

f Facebook.com/HarlequinBooks

y Twitter.com/HarlequinBooks

O Instagram.com/HarlequinBooks

P Pinterest.com/HarlequinBooks

ReaderService.com

EXPLORE.

Sign up for the Harlequin e-newsletter and download a free book from any series at **TryHarlequin.com**

CONNECT.

Join our Harlequin community to share your thoughts and connect with other romance readers! **Facebook.com/groups/HarlequinConnection**